D1740764

FIRST

CONTACT:

Book One of the Sloane Osborne Haunts for Sale Series

KAT GREEN

www.crescentmoonpress.com

First Contact
Kat Green

ISBN: 978-1-939173-94-2
E-ISBN: 978-1-939173-95-9

© Copyright Kat Green 2014. All rights reserved

Cover Art:
Editor: Kerry Genova
Layout/Typesetting: jimandzetta.com

Crescent Moon Press
1385 Highway 35
Box 269
Middletown, NJ 07748

Ebooks/Books are not transferable. They cannot be sold, shared or given away as it is an infringement on the copyright of this work.

All Rights Are Reserved. No part of this book may be used or reproduced in any manner whatsoever without written permission, except in the case of brief quotations embodied in critical articles and reviews.

This book is a work of fiction. The names, characters, places and incidents are products of the writer's imagination or have been used fictitiously and are not to be construed as real. Any resemblance to persons, living or dead, actual events, locale or organizations is entirely coincidental.

Crescent Moon Press electronic publication/print publication: July 2014 www.crescentmoonpress.com

CHAPTER 1

Waukesha, Wisconsin

Sloane Osborne desperately needed to find a haunted house.

Exactly two hours and thirty-three minutes to make contact before he would be gone forever.

Pausing on the rickety wooden steps of a house whose paint didn't quite match with the rest, she sighed before opening the lock box and retrieving the key. As one of the only paranormal real estate agents in the United States, it was part of her job. Search out haunted houses for people to purchase. An acquisition, of sorts, so they can say they own a haunted house.

What her clients didn't know was she was only searching for one ghost.

And tonight was her last chance.

This wasn't where she would have chosen to see him again. Why couldn't it have been a romantic bedroom in a classic Cape Cod style house lost in the windswept sands of coastal Maine? Instead, she was in Wisconsin of all places.

And it was hot. Wasn't Wisconsin supposed to be cold? July did that to the Midwest though.

Even this late at night, sweat dripped from her forehead, soaking her bangs and stinging her eyes. She brushed it away with a tired hand. She was already late. Her plane from Denver was delayed because of a storm. Tonight was not a night to be running behind. Still so much to do.

~ ☾ ~

The house didn't look like much. It was an average two story gable front with an enclosed front porch and two dormer windows peeking out off the roof. It strongly resembled the rest of the houses crammed onto the street. Only here, unlike the other houses, there were signs of wear and neglect. The gray paint was faded and cracked, the white trim peeling around the front door and windows. No, it wasn't much, but it was her last hope.

This ordinary house in nowhere Wisconsin was her last chance to make contact with Michael.

She knew it.

Michael Bain had been her fiancé.

Had been.

Past tense.

As in, they'd been driving to get their marriage license, just weeks before the wedding when a drunk driver smashed into them. She lived, he hadn't.

He'd always told her to be patient. If things weren't working, give it a year and a day to come out right. Try this job, but give it a year and a day. Let's move here, but just for a year and a day. It had always driven her crazy, but now it was her mantra.

Just before the squealing tires and crunching metal changed her life forever, he joked with her. Said if they didn't get their license today, they'd have to postpone the wedding. Call all their friends and family and tell them to save the date for a year and a day.

She hadn't had time to laugh.

And now she been waiting three hundred sixty five days, twenty-one hours and—she paused to glance at the Mickey Mouse watch he'd given her—twenty-eight minutes for him to come back and haunt her or to make contact. Though she'd always known he'd take a year and a day to do it, she smiled to herself. It was just like him to make her wait.

Sloane's paranormal research partner, Jonah

~ ☾ ~

Prescott, thought she needed help—psychiatric help—but he just didn't agree with her chosen profession. Michael and Jonah may have been best friends, the three of them doing everything together like some kind of bad sitcom, but his death was different for her. She didn't have any family to fall back on since her parents had died years before. Michael had been her family, best friend, and lover all rolled into one.

She still wore the engagement ring Michael had given her two years ago on Halloween. Couldn't take it off. That would mean admitting defeat and letting go completely and she wasn't ready for that. His spirit was out there somewhere. She knew it. He was waiting for her. She just needed to find him.

When Michael died, she was completely destroyed. It took a month for her to stop crying. Jonah had even staged an intervention. All he wanted was for her to get out of bed and take a shower. Instead he motivated her into a decision. She decided to stop waiting for Michael to come to her and to find him instead. She combined her recently acquired real estate license with her knowledge she gained in her paranormal group.

Jonah had informed her no one would pay to verify if a house was haunted before they purchased it. Boy, was he wrong. There were people out there who wanted to own haunted houses. Lots of people. They didn't always want to live there. One couple had actually called and said they wanted the prestige of being able to say "my summer home in Nantucket Bay, oh, it's haunted."

Since she started the website promoting herself as a paranormal real estate agent, she had more hits than she expected, but was waiting for a first sale. She needed to build up a reputation as a polite, respectful agent who happens to talk to ghosts before she got any real deals where they'd pay for her flight, accommodations, and enormous commission, of course.

He may not have believed in her but, as a good friend,

~ ☽ ~

Jonah helped. Sending her leads whenever he came across them. She usually followed his leads because he was everything she dreamed of being. He was a sensitive which meant he could see ghosts. According to him, he first saw a ghost just after his grandfather passed away. Jonah had come home from the funeral and found Grandpappy sitting on the front porch in his old rocker. He'd been able to see spirits ever since. He was seven at the time.

Sloane was still waiting for that first contact.

But she knew it would happen.

She found this job on her own, without Jonah's help. The contract came from a Mr. G.M. Spencer who was interested in purchasing this property as soon as possible, whether the house was haunted or not. It had thrown her when she got the email from the man, completely out of the blue. At first she didn't want to accept. For some reason, maybe it was how the email through her website was worded, but goose pimples crawled across her skin every time she so much as reread the short request for her expertise. But she really hadn't had a choice. She'd already blown through all of her savings and most of the wedding money she and Michael had saved.

The balance in her account was surprising, even to her, especially since she didn't do anything fun. She didn't date. She didn't go out. In fact, she was what was classically termed as someone with "delayed sleep phase disorder," which in English meant she was up at night and slept all day. Luckily that was her only vampiric tendency. But in her line of work, sleeping all day and working all night worked out perfectly.

That was one of the reasons she agreed to have him fly her halfway across the country. But mostly, it was timing.

Her year and a day were up so Michael had better be there.

There had been conflicting beliefs on whether or not

~ ☾ ~

this house was haunted. From the research Sloane had done, she knew no one was reported to have died in the structure. Up until six months ago the place had housed the same, original owner, for over fifty years. An old man who had just moved into a nursing home across town. Sloane had already spoken with the nurses but had yet to meet the man. From what she heard he kept to himself, was never married, and purchased the house just after a tour in Vietnam.

Not exactly the history she expected in her profession. There was usually a lot more murder and bloodshed with a haunted house.

Dumping her overnight bag and knock-off Coach purse just inside the door, she flipped on the switch. The dim, yellowy lights crackled to life with an audible hum. At least they worked and she wouldn't have to set up in the dark.

It didn't take long to walk through the house. It had a standard set up. The first floor consisted of a kitchen with a breakfast nook, a living area, a tiny den, and a half bath. The walls in every room were the same boring eggshell white. It made Sloane itch for a paintbrush and a splash of color.

The den was empty save for the deep gouges on the worn wood floor where furniture was removed. The other rooms were sparsely furnished: a small wooden table with two rickety chairs in the breakfast nook, a faded brown corduroy couch straight out of the seventies, and an outdated console television in the living room.

She couldn't resist stopping to switch on the old TV. Her parents had one of those when she was little but she hadn't seen one since they upgraded when she was seven. The set sputtered and a small circle of light appeared in the center of the screen, but no picture appeared. Flipping it off again, she headed upstairs.

There were two bedrooms and a full bath on the

~ ☾ ~

second floor. The attic above was hidden by a square wooden door in the ceiling with a frayed cord attached. Pulling the string released a set of creaky wooden stairs. She peeked into the attic, but it was empty. Nothing but dust, dirt, and eerie quiet.

Nothing about the house caused her anxiety. She wanted her heart rate to spike or chills down her spine but was disappointed.

The first bedroom wasn't much, just a desk in a corner and some books on a shelf. The bathroom was cramped with a claw-foot tub and pedestal sink.

The second bedroom had a brass bed, the scrollwork chipped and dented. It was made up in a faded flowered quilt, obviously handmade years before.

Sloane went back out into the hot evening air, pausing on the front porch to gaze out at the night. The moon was stark in the darkness and she stopped a moment to stare at the Cheshire cat smile it painted in the sky.

Turning to her rented Civic parked in the driveway, she was astonished—and admittedly a little put out—to see a man in a dark blue police uniform illuminated by the harsh streetlight peering into her vehicle. Why couldn't people just leave her alone? She only had one hour and forty minutes until midnight.

Still, it never hurt to be nice.

"Hello, officer. How are you tonight?" She asked as she came down the stairs.

Faded gray eyes and a flash of yellowed, crooked teeth in a cocky grin greeted her as the man turned. He looked to be around fifty with a thinning hairline and a body likely developed through years of drinking instead of time at a gym.

"My apologies, ma'am." His eyes perused her as he spoke. She knew what he saw. A pale faced twenty-something girl who was thin, but didn't work out. Long dark hair dropped half way down her back and what she

~ ☾ ~

liked to think of as her rock star bangs, stopping above her too big bright blue eyes. She wasn't used to being checked out—not anymore, at least since she was a hermit for the last year—but it was obvious he was enjoying the view.

"That's a lot of stuff you have back there," he continued.

"It's equipment." Refusing to be delayed, she moved past him to unlock the car.

"What kind of equipment?"

She reached past him to pull out the heavy case containing her electromagnetic field, or EMF, detector off the passenger seat.

"Paranormal equipment."

"You moving in here then?" he asked.

"I'm sorry. I should introduce myself." Reaching into the back pocket of her jeans she pulled out a worn, slightly bent business card. Not very professional but it was what she had. "I'm Sloane Osborne, Paranormal Real Estate Agent."

"I'm the sheriff in town. Name's Glen. Live right back there." He pointed to the house directly behind the one Sloane was investigating. "I was on my way home and I saw you out there on the porch." He smiled, reaching into the car for another bag. "The badge allows me to be nosey, I guess."

"Oh, so you're a neighbor as well as the sheriff?"

"Sure. Do you have a buyer? I've always been interested in this house, or at least my wife was. My Lily has been gone awhile now, but her dream was to tear down this house and have a fairy garden in our backyard. A place with lots of butterflies and a fountain and twinkling lights at night. When I saw the house was for sale I thought it was time to make her dream come true whether she was here or not."

"That's very noble of you." Sloane sighed. It was obvious the sheriff had really loved his wife. "I'm here

~ ☾ ~

working for a potential buyer but have to verify it's haunted but still safe for people before I can authorize the sale."

"Makes sense." He stared up at the house as though waiting for an apparition in a window. "My Lily, she always said there was something strange about the house. Gave her the chills just to look at it."

"Well, that's what I'm hoping for, Sheriff," Sloane agreed. "If it's haunted, I get paid so I'm hoping there are lots of ghosts tonight."

"Call me Glen." He smiled again, leaning over to pick up the heaviest of her bags. "Now, I'm not one to complain, but don't you have a partner or something to help you carry all this stuff?"

"I'd love a partner," she laughed. "I just haven't found the right person yet. You know, one who works for free."

"Then the least I can do is help you inside," he said.

"Well, Glen, if you can help me stack my things on the porch, you'd be a lifesaver. I can get them into the house."

They made quick work of her load, piling the boxes and bags on the front porch.

She thanked him for his help, then checked her watch as he pulled away from the curb. She still had forty-nine minutes.

She set up her equipment on the kitchen table, getting everything ready so she could grab it at a moment's notice.

Leaving the cases against the far wall under the only window in the breakfast nook, she set a static full-spectrum infrared video camera on a tripod and connected it to a separate digital video recorder which would record and monitor the video on an external monitor. She angled it so she could see the living room, the doorway to the den and the stairs. She left an audio recorder next to the ugly brown couch on top of the console and dropped a temperature sensor in the center

~ ☾ ~

of the room to record any drastic dips towards freezing that might indicate paranormal activity.

Once that equipment was set up it was time to really get to work. Flipping off the lights, Sloane did another walk through in the dark, using the infrared image on her video recorder as her eyes. She placed temperature sensors and audio recorders throughout the rest of the house. She would have liked another static video camera on the top floor but since she didn't have funds for a third device, she had to be content with keeping her handheld, along with her reliable K2 meter and SB7 ghost box with her at all times.

The K2 meter lit up both natural and paranormal sources of electro magnetic energy. If a number of lights came on steady and did not flicker, that was usually a natural source like an appliance, wiring, or a microwave. A paranormal source would usually cause two or more of the LED lights to flicker on and off. The more lights the higher the magnetic field. When it pegged to red, that was a hot source. Her ghost box provides a background white noise that spirits could manipulate to form words and sentences.

Hidden in the back of the kitchen pantry, she found a door she hadn't seen on her first walk through and realized there was a basement she hadn't searched before.

She ventured down the stairs. At the bottom of the steps, a thin string caressed her cheek and she pulled the cord. A single light bulb crackled to life, giving dim illumination to the room.

It was at least ten degrees cooler down here than the rest of the house, lending a welcome chill to the surroundings. Somewhere there was a leak and Sloane could hear the steady drip of water though she couldn't find the source. Odd but not uncommon.

The floor was a dull gray poured cement and the matching stone cement block walls were bare save for

~ ☾ ~

one small painting of a woman's face on the far wall. Across from the woman's picture was an incinerator. It looked homemade, constructed of dark red fireplace brick squared until it stood just a bit taller than her. The circular pipe vented from the top of the cube through a metal tube fit into the wall at the base of the foundation.

Out of curiosity, Sloane pulled the door to the incinerator. Even with her experience, she hadn't seen an incinerator like this before. It opened easily, sliding on well-oiled hinges. Inside was big enough for her to crawl right in. It would have been a tight fit, but possible. A strange thought, but it gave her an idea of how large it was and how much heat it would create. The inside chamber was pristine, as though recently cleaned. She could even see the shiny green finish on the heat-resistant tiling.

A lone mustard yellow recliner lounged under the picture. It was flush against the wall facing the incinerator with a round end table next to it. A small shot glass sat beside a half-full bottle of Hendricks Gin as though someone had set it there after taking a final sip.

The room smelled musty with a crisp charred scent like singed hair that gave Sloane pause. The incinerator looked too clean to be of use but perhaps the gentleman had taken extremely good care of it. With heating costs, she couldn't blame him.

She left some motion sensors and an audio monitor on the small table, careful not to touch the glass or the bottle. For a moment, she considered staying in the basement to get some readings, but decided to do another walk through. Glancing at her watch she headed upstairs. Seven minutes until midnight.

Her EMF readings were still between zero to zero point two around the house, spiking around electrical outlets, just like normal. Boring, in fact, and she was glad the coffee in her thermos was still piping hot when

~ ☾ ~

she got back to the kitchen where she left all of her equipment cases.

She walked the house again with her EMF and camera, looking for something—anything—that was different from before.

Nothing.

Not a blip out of place.

Deciding to try another tactic she returned upstairs to the digital audio recorder and thermometer.

Sadly, another walk through proved just as unsuccessful as the first.

Downstairs, she stopped in the center of the den and checked her watch again before sighing in defeat. It was almost midnight and Michael hadn't appeared.

What if he didn't come? What would she do then? Could she continue this kind of work knowing it was all in vain? That she might never see him again no matter what she did.

Would she even want to?

Then she heard it.

Banging.

Like a thousand hands knocking on the walls all around her.

Sloane's heart caught in her throat.

She glanced at her thermometer. The readings were the same. Nothing.

What was going on here?

Sloane's heart threatened to thump out of her chest. The knocking sounds echoed around her and she pivoted to figure out the direction the sound originated.

Had she finally made contact?

And if she had, where was Michael?

When she worked with her friend Jonah in the past, they'd been on excursions where ghosts had been sighted by members of her paranormal team, including Jonah. But if this was the real deal, it'd be the first time for her. According to Jonah, once a person managed to

~ ☾ ~

open a door to the spirit world and became a sensitive,
that door couldn't be shut.

Jonah had never told her whether he considered it a
curse or a blessing. Maybe she should have asked.

Everywhere she heard pounding.

Knock-knock. Knock-knock.

The sound reminded her of desperate people
pounding on the inside of their coffins after being buried
alive. Like dozens of people were trying to break through
the walls.

The first sliver of fear hit her and she pushed the
sensation firmly down into the pit of her stomach. No
time to be scared. The rapping grew louder and more
violent until her head pounded with the pain of ten
migraines. She covered her ears and sank to the floor
but not before she managed to switch on the Olympus
digital audio recorder stashed in her front pocket. As
soon as she hit the record button, the sound, which had
started so violently, faded and became faint and
rhythmic.

Well that sucked. It was as if the spirits *knew* she was
about to expose them.

But there was no doubt as to what she heard. After so
many failures, could she at long last be in a real haunted
house? "Hello?" she called. From the small den where
she stood, she closed her eyes to concentrate. "Is there
someone here who wants to talk to me?"

~ ☾ ~

CHAPTER 2

Staying perfectly still to create the least amount of atmospheric disturbance, Sloane mentally walked through the house in her head. Upstairs the two stuffy bedrooms and a cramped bathroom. The main level had the dank living room with the brown corduroy sofa. Her shoes scuffed the scratched up maple floors in the den where she now stood. Was she directly above that tattered recliner in the basement? The only other room on this level was the barren kitchen. All the rooms on the main level had windows covered with thick, dusty curtains.

Had the sound come from above or below her? She searched the place from top to bottom and rule out obvious reasons for the banging—rats under the stinky recliner or a giant colony of bats in the attic's crawl space. Even though neither could produce the kind of racket she heard.

The heaviness in her right hand had her glance at the digital recorder. When the knocking started, she'd clicked the record button. Popping out the mini USB cable, she downloaded the audio file to her PC which had powerful audio editing software that allowed her to detect EVPs much easier. No EVPs...like whatever was making the sound knew to stop.

Her Mickey Mouse watch moved his oversized white glove toward the midnight hour. Time was almost up— the year and a day was almost over.

C'mon Michael!

After one more sweep in the den with the K2 EMF

~ ☾ ~

meter that gave her a big, fat zero, Sloane padded over the wooden floors to grab her ghost box and video camera. She outfitted herself like a tourist on safari. Ghost box slung around her neck, K2 meter on her belt clip, and digital recorder on a black cord necklace, she switched on the viewfinder of the camcorder which became her eyes in the dark.

"Anyone here who wants to talk to me? Michael?" The same question hung unanswered in each room on the main level. No response. Mickey said there was less than ten minutes until midnight...until Michael was lost to her.

Stopping in the foyer, she spun around in a slow three-sixty.

Nada.

Her body slumped. No Michael and no evidence. Useless. Why had the knocking—which had been pounding like hammers—subsided almost the instant she began recording?

"Clearly, I'm going nuts," she said to no one. "Damn it!" Reasonable explanations wouldn't cut it for her on this investigation. "Argh! Give me something! Please!" She ached to connect with the dead. No, not the dead—with Michael.

The picture in her viewfinder cast a dim light. She traipsed once more upstairs to check for windows with loose shutters. A quick sweep upstairs wouldn't hurt before a final descent to the basement before the clock struck twelve.

Each stair her foot met emitted a groaning creak. With the playing card size view finder as her only set of eyes, oppressive heat pressed on her as she ascended. The trapped heat of the July night all rose to the second story. Perspiration dripped down the nape of her neck. Setting down the recorder, she retrieved a ponytail holder to secure her damp hair. Tucking the loose wispy curls that still clung to her cheek behind her ears, she let

~ ☾ ~

out a sigh. Michael loved to play with those escaped strands.

In the master bedroom, Sloane switched off her camera. More than enough moonlight streamed through the window. A rickety full metal bed frame and an antique dresser with an attached mirror were all that remained.

"What am I doing here?" She asked her reflection in the foggy mirror.

A face she didn't recognize stared back at her. It looked like death warmed over. Saggy eyes from lack of sleep. Lack of color from a face devoid of makeup. Was this the same girl Michael had wanted to marry? That anyone would ever marry?

The same girl who used to primp and preen for dates with her fiancé?

Empty eyes stared at her. When was the last time she cared about how she looked?

Oh yeah, the day she and Michael went to get their marriage license.

They'd planned to go get their marriage license then head out for an early dinner. Italian. Their favorite place where she would drink too much red wine and end up sharing her linguine in white clam sauce with Michael. The mouth-watering garlic bruschetta always filled her up.

She wore a lavender shirt and black tank with heels and even fussed with her hair, nails, and make-up.

"If I die first, I promise I'll haunt you," she'd teased him the last time they'd dined there. She wanted to demand the same from him. "And you—"

"Please do haunt me!" He interrupted her. "At least for a year and a day until I find myself a blonde!"

Sloane punched him in the shoulder.

Michael laughed, his eyes twinkling. "I'm kidding!" All at once, his face turned dark. "Hey, I've been meaning to tell you something. After we're married, no more ghost hunting."

~ ☾ ~

"Why not? You afraid one will follow me home?" She arched an eyebrow. They weren't even married yet and it sounded like he was not giving her an option here. She didn't like being told what to do. But a quiet voice told her Michael would be less controlling when wedding rings adorned both their fingers.

"Jonah can do it alone. He doesn't need you to be his partner."

"But—"

"I said no. Now tell me about that strawberry-filled wedding cake again..."

The memory faded.

After dating less than a year, Sloane had become obsessed with having the perfect wedding as soon as that ring had touched her finger. Like the vines creeping up a house, tendrils of doubt about their relationship were pushed aside so they could have the most romantic, perfect wedding day.

So in death—in the two seconds it took for him to die—Michael had been cast as the perfect man for her forever. No one would ever be able to compete with her memories and happily-ever-after what-ifs.

She jerked herself back into the moment to halt any more memories. Sloane hands formed clenched fists. She slammed them on the dresser and welcomed the pain that seared up her arms. Her tongue tasted the salt of tears and she heaved to catch her breath.

Pain was always preferable to emptiness.

"Michael!" she screamed at the empty room.

A piece of her still didn't believe he was dead. She refused to let him go.

"I hunt for one ghost, Michael. YOU!"

Stifling heat engulfed her. Needing some air, she crossed the room to the narrow double hung windows where moonlight poured in illuminating the room. She heaved on the handles but neither window would budge. No matter how hard she tried to wrench it open,

~ ☾ ~

nothing. A shoddy coat of paint coated the crevices essentially painting it shut. A quick glance outside where no shutters existed debunked her 'flapping shutters in the wind' explanation to the knocking.

Her flashlight confirmed the same paint job on the bathroom window.

In the spare bedroom, the paint cracked under Sloane's force. She managed to wrench it up. With no screen to barricade the starlit night air, she sank to her knees and stuck her head outside to gulp in fresh air. Evening primrose climbed the side of the house. Inhaling the sweet flowers and allowing the cool breeze to caress her face, Sloane felt her pulse slow and her neck and shoulders relax.

"Michael, just give me a sign that you're okay. Maybe then..." Her voice cracked and then her vision went cloudy with tears. This was why she refused to sleep. Every time she was fortunate enough to drift into a fitful slumber, Michael was her last thought. Every time she woke up, she still reached for him. It was killing her.

Wind whistled through the leaves of a massive oak tree in the neighbor's yard.

Mickey's gloved hand taunted her for the last time.

It was midnight, and nothing...

A year and a day was over. Time to give up her foolish idea of finding Michael in an old haunted house. The warmth of defeat coursed through her. Her mind whispered, *"You can curl into a ball sleep right here forever."*

But somewhere, her heart woke up. She wasn't a quitter—never had been. She was a fighter.

Dive into work. Forget about Michael. Investigate the knocking sound.

She cast one last look at the stars blazing overhead.

She exhaled after one last deep breath and reached for the handle to pull the window shut. "Good-bye, Michael."

~ ☾ ~

The scent of the primrose and blaze of the stars fell away. In a millisecond, all her senses went on high alert. Something, no someone, was in the room with her. Her body tingled and hummed.

Pressure on her shoulders...like hands. She screamed and tried to turn to see what it was. Something, or someone, held her in place.

She froze and fear trembled down her spine. Her next breath came out as a puff of smoke, like it did on a cold, winter day. She shuddered, realizing the temperature had plummeted.

On its own, the window edged downwards, creaking with each invisible adjustment. Her heart threatened to thump out of her chest. Wiggling and struggling, the hands held her firmly in place.

When the window slammed to a close, Michael was beside her in the pane's reflection.

Time stopped.

She felt the brush of his coarse hair against her cheek. She melted into his sea green eyes which were fixed on her. Time drifted backwards towards his rich citrus and pine scent. She knew the smell of his Hollister Jake cologne anywhere.

His lips moved. *"Find them."*

Sloane jumped up so fast that she slammed her head into the window. She spun around and scanned the room.

Nothing.

"Wait!" Scrutinizing the window pane and the mirror over the dresser, she willed him to re-materialize. "Come back!"

Her whole body shook. *That had been Michael!*

Wait. Had it? "Ghosts trick you, play games with you," Jonah had always said. "Most ghosts were humans once, but some are something else—sinister and dark."

If her desperation to connect with Michael had allowed her to let her guard down and open a portal to a

~ ☾ ~

dark entity, the consequences could be disastrous.

"C'mon! I'm right here! Talk to me. Find who?" She spun around trying to find a shadow, a cold spot, an orb of light...anything.

"How do I know you're really Michael anyway? Where have I always wanted to go?"

"Go see Mickey." Words spoken clear as day. The digital recorder—if it had been on—couldn't have missed that one.

She caught her breath. "Mickey! Michael, it *is* you!"

She checked the K2 EMF detector whose needle fluttered in the red zone.

And once again, the knocking started. Louder. More intense. From below.

No doubt this would be her first haunted sale! The lucky new owner would get woken up night after night by pissed off spirits banging on what? Invisible coffins? To Sloane, that would suck.

Knock-knock, knock-knock.

It was coming from the basement. She was certain now. The noise became urgent, as if time was running out.

With her heart in her throat and her sweaty palms barely able to hold her equipment, she made her way downstairs and stared at the rattling basement door. With a deliberate step forward, she reached out a trembling hand and turned the knob.

Before she could touch it, the whole door vibrated and shook, then burst wide open. The thrust threw her to the floor and sent her equipment flying. Icy wind blasted past her.

Cool concrete cradled her right cheek. Something pointy jabbed her ribs. The image of Michael in the window flashed in her mind like lightning from a summer storm. She was in the basement. Had she fallen down the stairs? Been pushed?

The drip-drip-drip of water echoed around her. Her

~ ☾ ~

work brain said to make a mental note to have the inspector look for a leaky pipe.

Peeling her cheek off the grainy floor, Sloane pulled her body to a sitting position. All her equipment was stacked neatly around her, except her K2 EMF recorder which was still on her belt clip and explained the pain in her ribs. She twisted her torso and moved each limb. No aches, no dire pain. And no broken bones.

She strained her memory. The basement door swung open. Then what?

Michael's words haunted her—literally. She flipped on her SB7 ghost box, which fast scanned either the AM band or the FM band. It could scan forward on each channel in the band selected or backwards. Scanning every channel on the AM or FM band and changing channels every 200 milliseconds made it impossible to pick up more than a syllable or two much less a full word from radio broadcasts. So when a full word or sentence was heard that was considered creditable evidence of a paranormal source. The familiar white noise soothed her. "Is anyone here?"

"Water." The pleading voice of a female came through the spirit box crisp and clear. Another voice spoke. Then another. All seemed to be asking for the same thing: *"Water."*

Goosebumps covered her entire body. She pulled herself to a standing position. Her K2 EMF detector was in the red zone. She placed the ghost box next to the whiskey on the end table. Lowering herself into the mustard yellow recliner, Sloane did the only thing she could... wait for more communication.

The position of the chair struck her as odd. It faced the homemade incinerator.

"Who needs water?"

White noise filled the room. The spirits were quiet.

She shivered, wishing she were on the couch in her apartment with her feet up and a blanket snuggled

~ ☾ ~

around her. Instead of watching Ghost Adventures, she was really in it!

"Yes!" The light on her digital recorder was red. It had been recording. She bolted upstairs with the mini USP cable, downloaded the files, and listened to her first raw evidence. *"Water."*

"Whoa." This was big. She captured intelligent electronic voice phenomena—EVPs! Evidence that would be hard to refute because there wasn't only one voice, but many, and simultaneously!

The female voices radiated heavy sadness and pain. Sloane couldn't stop the spirit's emotion from sinking deep into her own bones where it settled with a familiar feeling. Sadness and loss was something Sloane had grown comfortable with. The sinking feeling she held inside herself since the day Michael died, merged and tangled with these women's voices.

Tangible despair. Overriding pain fighting to overtake her. Sloane had to fight the feelings hard to stay vertical and functional. Embracing the anguish the spirits were giving off would have her drowning in the depths of unrecoverable depression.

Sloane squeezed her eyes shut and fought the feelings harder but the woman's voices seemed to consume her. Theirs was a different kind of pain... something hopeless and impossible.

Shaking away the dissimilarities between losing her fiancé and the sneaking suspicion that foul play had unfolded here, she let Michael's voice be her guide. He'd told her to find them and the hell if she would not only find these spirits, but help them move on if she could.

And she had help, because Michael was *here!*

Time to open up that incinerator. Back in the basement, the position of the recliner again struck her as odd. It sat facing the incinerator like it was a TV for watching. An odd scent hung in the air. Turning the metal handle, she peered inside. It contained none of

~ ☾ ~

the usual charred remains of paper and garbage. It was perfectly clean except for the strong scent of singed hair.

The meticulous cleaning, the smell, the position of the chair—it all pointed to one thing... murder. And before she could sell this house as "haunted by a harmless spirit", she needed to make sure that if innocent murdered spirits remained here, they got redemption.

Alvin Miller. At first light, she'd interview the former owner of the house. Next, she called in a favor to Jonah. He could check if the FBI or local PD had any missing person cold cases in this town.

With a firm plan for the next day and the house now quiet and past the witching hour, Sloane passed the next few hours in the recliner. No knocking. No voices. Even the dripping sound stopped. The needle on the EMF recorder refused to budge from zero.

She even dozed off here and there.

Before leaving at 6:00 a.m., she sank to her hands and knees for a more nook and cranny view of the basement. She crawled and examined each cool surface of the basement meticulously. The early morning sun brightened the clear glass block windows. Finding nothing unusual or out of place at ground level, Sloane got up and went to examine the sole picture hung in the room.

A woman. The snapshot had been taken from across the street of a mousy haired young woman whose fuzzy profile was traversing a city sidewalk. Alvin's wife? Or one of the spirits that spoke to her last night?

After packing her equipment in the rental, she headed out the front door and squinted in the blinding morning light. The nearest motel took her soon-to-be-maxed-out credit card as a deposit and after hauling her equipment into the room, Sloane looked at the bed and yawned. Her idea of going to see Alvin first thing, without any sleep, seemed foolish.

~ ☾ ~

The paisley polyester comforter called to her and all at once, her trip to see Alvin was postponed till mid-morning, along with combing past police and newspaper reports. Sloane peeled off her jeans, socks, and running shoes and pulled on shorts before collapsing under the crisp white sheets. When sleep beckoned, as it rarely did, Sloane was happy to comply.

Her head hit the pillow and she welcomed fitful slumber.

She had her same recurrent dream.

Of Michael.

She was cradled in his arms. He headed toward the surf, bare feet crunching in the white sand beach. She wore her flowing silk wedding dress and he had on a loose unbuttoned white, linen shirt and dress pants. She laced her fingers around his neck and squeezed, never wanting to let go. His footing became less sure and she looked down to see he'd walked right into the crashing waves. Her toes got wet, splashed by the cold waves.

He gently untangled her arms and released her. His face was serene. Panic overtook her. "What are you doing? We're too far from shore!"

He let her go. She forgot how to swim! Kicking her legs did nothing, the ocean pulled her down. She swallowed water but bobbed to the surface. Desperation made her thrash her arms and legs trying to reach Michael. He only watched. When she was almost able to touch his fingertips, he suddenly disappeared and then his apparition reappeared far away on the shoreline. "Michael!" she screamed, flailed her arms. "Don't let me go! Help me!"

She thrashed in the water trying to swim toward him but every stroke took her farther out to sea. Sinking. Drowning. She gasped for breath.

Screaming his name and tangled in the motel comforter, Sloane woke up on the floor of the cheap motel in a heap, tears streaming down her face.

~ ☾ ~

CHAPTER 3

After three cups of coffee and a stale donut in her motel room, Sloane was ready for work.

Firing up her computer, Sloane debated whether to send the buyer a note about the house or wait until she knew more. She had to let him know that, in good faith, she could not sell the house now. It wasn't safe and she wouldn't sell it until it was.

She knew she should be overjoyed with the proverbial jackpot of ghosts she hit but questions nagged at her. Her incessant curiosity had always been her downfall. It could be something as simple as an old family burial ground that had been disturbed when the subdivision had been built, but she still wanted to know for sure. It was a mystery and she always loved a good mystery.

She started by Googling the town on her laptop. It was more interesting than she expected. Waukesha had nothing unusual—three high schools, a couple of colleges, and she knew where to call if she wanted to report a pot hole. It was also the birthplace of Les Paul, and the home of the BoDeans. Used to be a sought after spring water site, and had been one of the missile batteries during the Cold War.

Unexpected things really did happen in sleepy towns.

There were Native American burial mounds by the library and local university. She could even learn who'd just been buried in the local cemetery, but there wasn't anything about the subdivision and the house she'd been in last night.

~ ☾ ~

Leaning back in the hard wooden desk chair, she chewed on the tip of her pen as she ran scenarios through her mind. No history for the house. No burial mounds. Just an empty house with a large incinerator and girls asking for water and Michael telling her to find them.

A sick image flashed in Sloane's head of an emaciated body slumped at the base of a hole, head turned to the side. She seemed to cry without tears, her lips chapped and blistered, eyes glazed with pain. Clear as a bell, she heard the word whispered in her head again.

Water.

It would be a horrible way to die.

But had anyone died that way?

And was there a way for her to find out?

Jumping to her feet so fast her legs bumped the wobbly table she almost knocked her laptop to the floor. Sloane picked up her phone and dialed the number without thinking.

He picked up on the third ring, but her heart hadn't slowed.

"When I told you to call whenever, I didn't expect that to be in the middle of a workday. I do have a job besides being the greatest guy you know, Sloane."

His tone made her smile, though she had to bite her lip to keep herself from crying. Jonah Prescott had been Michael's best friend since kindergarten. She had trouble thinking about one without the other. Yet, there he was, going on with life, while Michael was gone. This was why she didn't call him anymore. Not unless it was an emergency.

"And some of us have jobs that aren't cushy FBI government jobs, thank you very much. I happen to be working right now."

"Really?" He wasn't really paying attention. Listening but not. She could hear the papers flipping on his desk as he probed into a file. He was probably more focused

~ ☾ ~

on his newest case. Jonah worked cold cases. And he was good at solving them.

"Really. Just found a house full of ghosts in Wisconsin and I was..."

"Wisconsin?" He didn't let her finish. "I sent you a lead on a house in Virginia. Nothing in Wisconsin. Why the hell would you go there?"

She chuckled at the edge in his voice. He'd always thought of himself as her protector, even when Michael was alive. It was nice to know some things hadn't changed.

"I am capable of finding jobs on my own Jonah. Just because you were Michael's best friend, that doesn't mean you have to take care of me."

He paused and she heard him sigh. She knew just how he'd look. A little frazzled, not quite comfortable in the suit the job required. Dark hair messed from running his hand through it like he was probably doing now.

"I know. I know. But you were my friend too and I worry about you. Why didn't you take my lead? I know what I'm talking about."

"Yes, yes, I know. Mr. I-saw-my-first-ghost-at-seven, but this was my lead. My chance to make contact. And I did."

She waited for his reaction but the line was quiet. Not even the sound of him fumbling with papers on the other end.

"With *him* or with a ghost?" His voice was so quiet she could barely hear.

"Both."

"You mean you saw Michael? Tell me everything."

It didn't take as long as she thought. She didn't leave out a single detail, not even that she couldn't remember how she gotten to the bottom of the stairs to the basement. She even told him about the cold fingers that had crept down her spine when she envisioned the girl

~ ☾ ~

dying at the bottom of the hole. When she finished, Jonah was quiet but she could hear his fingernails tapping on the edge of his keyboard as he thought.

"So you're sure there was more than one voice?" he asked when she finished.

"I have them on tape, Jonah. They're all speaking together but you can clearly hear more than one."

She stayed quiet while she heard his fingers working over his keyboard.

"And the incinerator. You said it was clean."

"Like it was new or something. I could even see the green tile."

He was quiet again. Too quiet for too long.

"Well..." she prompted.

"Well what?" he asked.

"Most of the time you think you have all the answers so I thought I'd use that to my advantage for once," said Sloane.

"What do you want me to say?" he asked. "Do you want me to tell you it was a good job? You did a good job. I'm proud of you. But you're in over your head. I'll have clearance to be there by the end of the day?"

"What, no... you don't need to come here," she insisted. "This is my house. My sale."

"I'm not going to sell the house for you, Sloane. I'm going to help you figure out what happened there."

"So I'm right. You think there's something going on?" she asked.

"I'm telling you to stay put in that hotel room. Don't even think about going back to that house and stay away from the previous owner. I want to talk to him first."

"You want the glory," she teased.

"No. That won't work for me." He sounded tired. "I need to know you're safe. Now promise me you'll stay where you are."

She bit her lip, knowing what she was going to say and knowing what his reaction was going to be. He was

~ ☾ ~

always too possessive. She didn't belong to him. She
never had.

"I promise you I'll be careful." It was the only
compromise she could come up with.

His breath hitched and she knew he was mad.

"I guess that's the best I'll get, isn't it?" He sighed and
she could swear she heard his heart in his voice. "Just
know that if anything happened to you, I wouldn't
recover. Can you remember that?"

"Jonah, don't..."

"No, I'm serious. I've already lost my best friend.
Don't make me lose you too."

"I'll be careful." She promised. "And I'll see you soon.
Bye, Jonah."

Slone closed her eyes, pressing the phone against her
chest. If Jonah was insisting she wait for him, then he
was right. As much as she didn't want to admit it, she
probably was in over her head. But he was coming. She
felt a little thrill run through her. She hadn't seen him in
months. It would be good to see him. Sad, but good.

Opening her eyes, she smiled. He wanted her to stay
in her hotel room until he got there? Fat chance. He
didn't want her to go to the house or to see the previous
owner? Well, that was exactly what she was going to do
as soon as she verified his visiting hours.

And she wasn't even going to feel guilty about it. After
all, it had been his idea.

There wasn't anything outwardly disturbing about
Alvin Mitchell, but the moment Sloane entered his
private room at the London Oaks nursing home behind
the nurse on duty, the fine hairs on the back of her neck
stood on end. He was small and wiry, like Gollum in the
Lord of the Rings, with wispy white hair and cool blue
eyes deep set in a weathered face. He appeared frail, as
though his bones could no longer hold the weight from
his slender frame.

"Time for your evening pills, Mr. Mitchell." The

~ ☾ ~

young nurse hurried to the bed to help him sit, fluffing the pillows behind him.

"Already that time again? How about we skip the pills tonight, Becky, and instead we take a ride, you and me. You can bring your sister." He glanced over at Sloane, his red-rimmed eyes twinkling.

"My sister? You know I don't have a sister, Mr. Mitchell," the nurse glanced back at Sloane. "I've brought you a visitor."

"So Becky is here to bring me my pills, and you're the sugar to help them go down. What a night made in heaven."

His flirting seemed harmless but something deep down told Sloane not to engage him.

"You're shameless, Mr. Mitchell." The nurse twittered. She actually twittered. Sloane wouldn't have thought it possibly if she hadn't heard it herself. "This nice young lady is Miss Osborne. She's here to ask you some questions about your old house. She's the real estate agent."

Alvin swallowed the pills the nurse handed him, waving away the water she offered him in a Styrofoam cup with a plastic lid and bendy straw. Sloane cringed. She never understood how people could take pills without water. She was certain she would choke.

"Miss Osborne," he turned on the bed so he faced her. "It's so nice to have a visitor. Come in. Take a seat." He patted the bed beside him as if she would actually choose to sit there. "What can I do for you?"

Sloane had always thought people in homes like this were on the verge of death and couldn't take care of themselves. When she first saw Alvin from the doorway, she would have said he was exactly that. But when Nurse Becky left the room, his demeanor metamorphosed into a completely different man. He sat up straighter, his light blue eyes brightening as he smiled at Sloane.

~ ☾ ~

She politely returned his smile as she took a seat in the small slat-backed chair furthest from him. Sloane placed her purse in her lap and returned the level gaze of the man who was eyeing her with more interest than she liked.

"I was wondering if you'd be willing to tell me anything about the history of your old house?" she asked.

"Ah, my home. I miss that place. You have no idea how much. What would you like to know?" His eyes twinkled. Sloane got the impression that he had information about the house he'd love to tell her if he could.

"Has anything unusual ever happened there?" Sloane asked.

"Define 'unusual.'" If possible, the old man's smile got even bigger as he watched Sloane. She got the impression he was toying with her and decided to just cut to the chase and get to the point of the conversation.

"All right. To me unusual would be the knocking coming from behind the walls and the voices in the basement. Have you heard either of those?"

"What kind of voices?" he asked, though he smiled eerily at his own question.

Sloane played the EVP she'd captured from a file she'd sent to her cell phone. Agonizing voices pleading for water. She watched Alvin, looking for any reaction. From the way his smile widened, Sloane knew he'd heard the voices before.

"You've heard the knocking too, haven't you, Alvin?"

"Of course I've heard them knocking, heard them calling for help. I've heard everything they've ever said. My home has been haunted for a very long time."

Sloane had a sinking feeling he'd heard those voices before their souls had left this world.

"Do you know if there was ever a cemetery or burial ground under where your house is now?" she asked.

~ ☾ ~

"No, I don't believe so." Alvin shifted forward in this chair. "Can I hear that again?"

She pressed play again. Sloane watched him closely, noticing the way his eyes brightened as he heard the desperate plea.

"You're sure it wasn't a graveyard of some sort?"

"I'm sure," he said. "Why would you ask?"

"It's the only thing I could think of to explain how there could be so many voices in one house. Usually hauntings are one ghost, not many held in the same space."

"How many do you think there were? Maybe we should listen again?"

It was an odd question. She played the EVP a third time. Sloane counted at least seven different voices calling out for water. Possibly more.

What really caught Sloane off guard was the look of— was it pride?— in Alvin's eyes.

"How many did you hear?" she asked.

Alvin turned his head away from her to stare out the one window at the view of the parking lot. Sloane waited, sure he had something to say.

"Let me tell you a story." He said after a minute. "When I was young, well younger than I am now, I met a beautiful woman. She was lovely. The picture of perfection with long dark hair and shining blue eyes." He leaned forward, his eyes squinting as he looked Sloane over. "Actually, she looked a little like you. Anyway, I fell in love with her. But love is a fickle thing. It doesn't always work the way you'd expect it to. Do you know that, Miss Osborne? Have you ever lost someone you loved?"

"I have."

"I knew it the moment I saw you. You have that look about you. Experience, I call it. But back to my story. This woman was everything to me and I would have lassoed the moon, if that's what she wanted me to do. I

~ ☾ ~

would have done anything. That kind of love is a once in a lifetime thing, you know."

Sloane nodded because she did know what he was talking about. This one thing they did, indeed, have in common. She would have done anything for Michael and she'd do anything to have him back. And she could see from the dreamy look in his eyes, that Alvin had loved and he'd lost, as she had.

"There's a picture of her down in the basement," he continued. "Only one I have left of her."

"I saw that picture. She was, indeed, very beautiful."

"But the problem is that she didn't love me back. My beautiful Karen made me love her but would not love me in return. Can you imagine that? It's a horrible thing. And I couldn't live knowing she didn't love me. I just couldn't."

"So what did you do?" Sloane asked.

"What do you think I did?" He raised a mocking eyebrow.

Any sane and normal person would have cried, had some chocolate marshmallow ice cream, watched some old sappy movies and gotten over it. But Sloane was beginning to suspect that wasn't even close to what Alvin had done.

"I'm afraid to tell you what I think you did."

"You're a smart girl," Alvin sighed. He suddenly looked old again. Slowly, as though in pain, he lay down on the hospital bed again, curling onto his side so he could still look at her. "Smarter than most."

"Was she your only love?" Sloane asked.

"I admit, it took me a long time to get over her, but I did find someone else."

Sloane bit her lip trying to decide what to ask next.

"I'd like you to find them, you know?" He yawned, though his eyes were bright.

"Find who, Alvin?"

"My girls." He closed his eyes as though tired of the

conversation and rolled away from her to face the wall.

"You mean Karen?"

His only response was the soft sound of his snoring.

"Were there others?" Sloane stood, moving closer to the bedside as though drawn there by an invisible cord.

"Many," he said, pulling his sheet up around his thin frame.

Sloane was stumped. Was this man a wolf in sheep's clothing or a crazy old man?

His chest rose and fell as Sloane waited, knowing she should leave but unable to make herself go. She still had so many questions. Shifting her weight from foot to foot she hovered over his bed, trying to decide if she should let him sleep or try to rouse him for another round of questions.

Alvin grunted, the sound almost annoyed, then turned quickly to face her, his eyes open to angry slits. Whatever radiated off this man was not cotton candy and rainbows.

"Miss Osborne," His voice was harsh and low. "We both know my home isn't haunted. You will not find anything, but go ahead..."

~ ☾ ~

CHAPTER 4

Sloane sat in her beat up Civic staring intensely at the manicured emerald lawn outside Alvin's nursing home. "It's a Small World" piped up from her cell phone. "Uh-oh," she winced seeing Jonah's caller ID. He'd give her a lecture about going to see Alvin without him.

Best to fess up to the feds.

She flipped the phone open. "Hello."

"Hi ya." Jonah's deep, throaty voice filled her head. "I trust you stayed in your hotel room and are patiently waiting for me, right? I'm at the airport in D.C.."

Sloane rolled her eyes.

"Don't roll your eyes at me."

"How did you?—Seriously, Jonah." I guess this is why he was good at his job, his ability to read people. "Look, about going to see Alvin..."

A low groaning ensured on the other line. "You didn't! I don't know what it is, but I have such a bad feeling about that guy."

"Yeah, sorry. I kinda did go see him."

Sloane let the silence fill the air.

"Fine, fill me in. Details, please."

Sloane summarized their interview making sure to tell him about his obsession with her replaying the EVP session and talking about his lost love Karen. She waited for Jonah's response. "Well?"

"I need to digest your info. You know I'm not a rash decision maker."

Sloane did know. From their long nights doing investigations together, she learned that when he wasn't

~ ☾ ~

speaking, that usually meant he was rolling a million things around in his head. And eating. The man was always eating.

"Well first off." She was right. He was chewing, "I can't believe you went to see this old nut job alone. How many times have I told you never to do an investigation alone? Hire a partner already!" He gulped.

"Do you really need a Big Mac to digest this information? You can be my partner because I'd only be able to pay you in Happy Meals." The rustling and chewing continued on the other end. "You know I have no money yet to hire a partner. But I will. Hey, did anyone ever tell you McDonald's isn't a food group."

"When you say cruel things like that to me, I almost want to cry. The airport McDonald's in D.C. adds another secret ingredient to their secret sauce." More chomping and swallowing. "Now give me a minute. I'm thinking."

"You mean chewing," she laughed. "But I know how you operate. Take your time.

Wait. Why are you at the airport?"

"'Cause I'm catching the next flight to Milwaukee. What is that? Like a half hour from Waukesha?"

"Wait, you're really coming here? Alone?" The word came out wrong. But Jonah had better not be bringing his stick-up-her-perfect-ass blonde FBI partner he'd been assigned to work with just after Michael died and he'd had the audacity to bring her to Michael's funeral.

"I *was* going to come alone, but maybe I should call my partner. And while I do the real work you can tell her knock-knock jokes over martinis and some mani-pedis." He paused busting out laughing at his own joke.

"You're hysterical for a man who preaches equal rights for women."

"Sheesh Miss Doesn't-Listen to her FBI advisor, you know I'm kidding."

Her heart sank at the idea of the buxom beauty

~ ☾ ~

getting coffee with him every morning and chasing bad guys after lunch. Why was she thinking that? Jonah was her friend and that was all. Where were these emotions coming from? "I got one for her. Why can't you tell blondes knock-knock jokes?"

"Why?" Jonah appeased her.

"Because they go answer the door."

He snickered and a pencil scraped paper on the other end.

"Writing that one down?"

"You know it.

More scribbling. "Look Jonah, it might be nothing. And for you to fly all the way here..."

Jonah wasn't a leader or a follower. He was a watcher. The man had the gift of being able to see everything going on around him at all times. In addition to his attuned paranormal senses, even minute details never escaped him. He could walk into a bar and immediately tell you how many people were packing, which girls were looking to get laid, and how long the bickering couple had before they called it quits.

He'd once told Sloane he kept his mind always switched on high and his heart on low. "Self-preservation" was the righteous bullshit term he used to explain his mad methods of survival. Jonah was born to be FBI and his life's work had always been to protect people.

That's probably why Michael's death had hit him so hard. He hadn't been able to do anything to stop it.

"Sloane, if you say something is not right, I believe you. I feel it too." His voice was lowered, more serious. "And I've already pulled the missing persons cases in Waukesha County, Wisconsin. I've set up a meeting with the local PD. As the FBI cold case guy, this is now my jurisdiction. I want to know more about Alvin saying, 'Karen and my girls.' Found a good diner for us to chat at yet?"

~ ☾ ~

The idea that he was hours away from having coffee with her melted the tension in her neck. Relief. She hadn't realized how much she missed him until she knew she was going to see him again. "I'll get on it. Anything to improve on your regimen of fast food," she laughed.

"Your favorite blonde already put Alvin through the FBI database. Squat. I'll check the town's cold case files for anyone named... what was it?"

"Karen," she reminded him. "I'll take a picture of the photo in his creepy basement with my phone and send it to you."

"Sloane, I am happy to cease and desist all my current FBI assignments posthaste to check out this old dude in a nursing home if you promise me one thing."

"What's that?" She asked.

"Get a damn partner! And stay away from that house until we know more." His tone sounded like more of an order than a request.

"I'll get on the partner thing. But I can't promise I'll stay away from the house. You won't be here in time and I have to go see if he shows..." She stopped. "I have to go see if the knocking happens again. And Jonah?"

"Yeah?" he answered, his voice husky.

"Thanks for still worrying about me. It feels nice." Although Sloane forced herself to accept change, maybe better than most people, still being able to count on Jonah was comforting.

"Anytime, Sloane. Anytime."

She clicked her phone shut and cruised Main Street until she found a diner. She spread out her notes on the freshly wiped-down tabletop of a corner booth.

"What can I getcha?" A raspy-voiced waitress asked, pad of paper and pencil at the ready.

"Just coffee please, black." No Starbucks in this joint. Her name tag said "Marge" and her grey tied-back hair

~ ☾ ~

and creased face indicated this job was her bread and butter. "Thank you."

Sloane's thoughts drifted to Jonah. She hadn't seen him since Michael's funeral. After the funeral, Jonah built walls around him that were soaring and double-steel reinforced. Besides Michael, he never *really* let anyone in. But Sloane had glimpsed the real Jonah during their paranormal investigations. What lay under his cocky exterior was a dark haired, smoky eyed savior who would go out of his way to save a damsel in distress or even something as small as helping a turtle about to be run over on the road.

Compassion. Real, honest-to-goodness, I – put – others – above – myself – and – expect – nothing – in – return ... compassion. She knew it was there. But he hid that person from the outside world.

****

Every dusty piece of glassware in Alvin's house was filled with tap water and moved to the basement. It now surrounded her like a protective circle. If the ghosts wanted water, water they would get. A yawn escaped and she rubbed her eyes. Darkness fell hours ago and there was zilch on the K2 EMF detector.

She pushed the button for "hit" on a three of heart and Queen of spades on the blackjack game on her cell. Nine of hearts. Bust. "Guess I should stay away from Vegas until Zak Bagans himself invites me." Sloane laughed at her own joke.

She shifted her position in the basement's ratty recliner. The full spectrum video camera was now set up in the corner. Check. Trigger finger ready on the digital audio recorder. Check. After hours of nothing, Sloane began to wonder if last night had been a figment of her imagination.

Mickey hit 3:00 a.m. All at once and out of nowhere—BOOM—BOOM—BOOM. All hell broke loose... again.

The jolting noise made covering her ears was the

~ ☾ ~

priority and her recorder bounced when it landed on the floor. The banging pierced her like a gong reverberating through every cell in her body, hammering assaults from every direction. She wished she was back upstairs as this was obviously the source of the noise. Ground zero.

Her heart kept beat with the racquet pounding from every direction. The water in the glasses shook like an earthquake was about to rip the house apart.

"Stop!" she screamed. "I hear you! What do you want?" No doubt about this place being haunted now. Something heavy seemed to press in around her from every direction. Suffocation by spirits.

Just as fast, the pressure and the banging stopped. She scooped up the digital audio recorder from the floor and hit the on/off switch. Good, not broken. She waved at the red light on the static video camera set up on a tripod in the corner of the room. "Who is here with me?"

"We are." Invisible voices answered from every direction. "Get out," said one. "Not safe," said another.

Wow! More class A EVPs! Sloane stood, carefully stepping over the water and circled the perimeter of the room trying to figure out where the next spirit voice would come from. "Why don't you want me here? What's not safe?"

Squat. Zilch. Nada.

Stinking ghosts only telling you what they want.

"Is Karen here?" She asked, trying out her new piece of information.

A bang behind her. She jumped and spun around. The picture of the woman was on the floor face down. Light knocking resumed, from *behind* that wall where the picture had hung.

Sloane reached down and brushed off the dusty picture. "Hi Karen," she said, hanging it back on the wall.

As soon as she released her hand from the frame, it began to sway.

~ ☾ ~

"Holy shit," Sloane muttered while backing up.

Then the dead began to materializing from the wall, one by one.

The first one that caught Sloane's eye was a girl, no more than eighteen years old. She had matted dark hair, hollow eyes, and a gaunt face. She wore a sheer nightgown. The next one was a bit older, drool escaping from her chapped lips, and arms outstretched to Sloane, and not in a warm, fuzzy way. Matted hair covered most of her face. "*Water*," she drawled, more of a command than a request.

The images flickered, appearing then reappearing elsewhere. The girls all resembled the photograph of Karen in some way. Damn, the person who did this was a sicko.

One after another, they appeared. Sloane counted six. Desperation oozed from them and gnawed at and seeped into Sloane who stood frozen. In shock. Four more appeared. Then two behind them. All women. Their lips and faces cracked and peeling. They all said the same thing... *water*.

The glasses of water on the ground shook, then one by one, spilled or smashed. The water cascaded toward the drain, untouched. She gotten them water but it appeared they were going to be denied, even in death.

So much for the peace offering.

Sloane backed up until her hands met cool concrete. She was pressed against the wall near the stairs.

None of the girls paid her any attention, trying in vain to get the glasses. Black rage filled her mind. She tasted bile in the back of her throat as her stomach turned with revulsion at the horrible images flashing in front of her. Had they been held in this basement? Tortured? Incinerated? Died of thirst?

"Who did this?" Sloane demanded.

One by one, they raised their head and looked right at her.

~ ☾ ~

Before Sloane could locate a bucket, she puked all over the cement floor.

All of their attention was focused on her. Images flickered and flashed. They were getting closer. Hands outstretched. Sloane couldn't move. Her fear had her frozen in place.

"Help," she whispered to no one as the mob approached.

Backing towards the staircase, the hollow-eyed black-haired girl reached her first. A razor sharp pain of searing heat hit her arm when the girl touched her. She screamed and the girl disappeared.

"More water," the next girl said, crying with eyes that were too dry to shed tears.

Sloane managed to edge up the staircase. Time to get the hell out of Dodge. Three more ghosts emerged from the far wall. Sloane crept backwards up two more steps toward the relative safety of the house above.

One of the girls lurched forward, catching her foot. With pale flaking skin and sunken cheeks, the ghost's hand held her ankle like a vice grip. *"Leave. You're next."*

Vacant eyes and sunken faces surrounded her.

"Get out."

"Don't come back!"

"Let me go! I can help you!" Sloane's head swam and her vision tunneled. On the verge of passing out from lack of oxygen, suddenly a bright light pierced the darkness from the top of the staircase. The girls covered their eyes and scattered, screaming before being sucked behind the same walls from where they'd emerged.

The knocking began again like the girls were immediately trying to get back out.

The light was so bright that at first, Sloane couldn't look at it. But she didn't have to. She knew what it was. Or rather *who*. She could sense him. Just like in the upstairs bedroom.

~ ☾ ~

Michael.

Crawling up the stairs toward the light, she forced her eyes open, ignoring the persistent knocking from behind her.

The ethereal shape at the top of the stairs had Michael's perfect face. Strong cheekbones, crooked nose, tousled hair and eyes that... eyes that weren't the same. No depth, no...life.

This was Michael's spirit, not Michael. But it was still the visage of the man she loved. He held up his transparent hand. *"Quiet!"* The knocking stopped. *"Sloane, you're not safe here. Go."*

Her body tingled with excitement and her heart swelled. With the aid of the railing, she took the steps two at a time and tried to jump into his arms. The only thing that caught her was empty air.

He was gone.

She slumped down on the top stair. The sunken faced women began reemerging from the walls.

"Michael, don't go," was the only thing she could choke out through a veil of tears.

She ached every day to see his playful grin directed at her. In life, Michael had had a light within him. In death, that light of his spirit glowed around him.

"I never left you. I never really will." He stood at the bottom of the stairs.

Her feet carried her once again to where he stood. To the safety of his arms. But she ended up in the arms of one of the ghost girls. Repulsed, she screamed and retreated backwards.

Why could they have substance when Michael could not? Sloane instinctively jabbed an elbow into the girl's chin, turned and fled up the stairs. She stumbled at the top but never looked back when she rammed through the basement door, through the empty front hall and outside in the crisp night.

The huge gulps of air did nothing to calm her nerves.

~ ☾ ~

The wind rustled through the oak trees and wisps of moonlight striped the sidewalks and lawns. Sweat dripped down her back. Her body shook. But it wasn't just the night air making her cold.

Someone was walking towards her.

From behind a row of thick shrubs, Alvin's neighbor, the sheriff strolled up to her wearing a t-shirt and shorts and chugging ice water from a bottle. "Find a black hole in that house or something?"

"Glen!" Sloane grabbed onto him like a life rope and he caught her before she sank to her knees.

"Are you okay?" he pressed.

"What?" Sloane's mind spun and she couldn't focus her eyes. She stared at a tear in her pants until her vision refocused. "The basement..." She blinked and concentrated on his grey eyes which appeared to be on alert. "Just had some contact with the other side I think."

Glen laughed. "Whoa... a ghost, really? That is incredible!"

Sloane pulled herself to her feet after shaking off his assistance. "Ghosts. As in plural."

"Tell me how I can help you? Did you get video?" He paused and furrowed his brow at her shaking form. "I'm sorry. You look pretty shook up. Do you need a ride to your hotel? You don't appear to be in any shape to drive. I have the squad."

She shook her head and her cell rang from inside her pants. She held up a finger to Glen. He mouthed, "Ok. Stop over when you're done. I'll be next door if you need anything," and headed home.

Jonah's number flashed on her caller. "Hey." She tried not to sound like she'd just had a close encounter with her fiancé and Jonah's best friend.

"Twenty-six women have disappeared over the last few decades in that town. All cold case files. Something smells wrong about that town. Get out of that house until I get up there."

~ ☾ ~

"Twenty-six huh? I'm out of that house, Jonah. But the girls' ghosts are pissed and all roaming around in Alvin's basement. You can bet I won't go back in there unless you're with me. But I am going to talk to Mr. Mitchell again."

"Sloane, I don't think..."

She hung up before he had time to respond.

"So you're kind of a sick fuck, huh?"

Alvin Mitchell smiled at Sloane with a face of stone while he sipped his noon time applesauce.

"How'd you kill them?"

"Feel free to ask them," he leaned toward her, "before you join them."

"Right, you're a big bad murderer sitting here in an adult diaper in an old folk's home. You set up for bingo later? How are the golden years treating you? Why don't we just get this on the table and you can clear your conscience to me before you go to hell for being a sick bastard?"

Alvin pulled a handkerchief from his shirt sleeve and coughed heavily into it. If he'd murdered anyone in that house, it was a while ago based on his limited physical abilities and declining health. The white cotton was spotted with fresh and dried blood when he crumpled it up and shoved it back inside his sleeve. His eyes shone as he looked Sloane up and down. "Ever suffered a day in your prissy ass life, Ms. Osborne?"

"Not as much as you're going to suffer when you rot in hell, Alvin." Sloane gave him a fake grin. "Tell me the names of your victims so I can let those spirits get some rest."

"There is no hell, just hell on earth." Alvin backed up his wheelchair and reached for his water glass. He slurped the liquid through a straw with a shaky, age-spot ridden hand. "The latest girl isn't so dead. Can you still smell her?"

~ ☾ ~

Sloane took a deep breath and unclenched her balled fists.

She envisioned snatching him off his wheelchair and throwing him down flights of stairs until he gave her answers. This old man couldn't be a threat to her.

Self-preservation kicked in. The man had information in his deranged head she needed to extract. But he might not be able to answer her questions if he was unconscious.

Sloane crossed her arms and leaned against the wall. "You talking about Karen or are you talking crazy?"

"I am not crazy." A haze passed over his face and he once again looked like a tired, old man.

A chunky woman in a grubby teal scrubs gave a quick knock on the door. "Time for your bath." she said, her voice the deep rasp of a heavy smoker.

She released the lock on his wheelchair and headed for the bathroom. Alvin put a hand on the doorframe to stop them before he disappeared into the bathroom. He cast a Sloane a sharp-eyed look. "Go ahead and keep looking, Ms. Osborne. Good luck with that. As I said, the day you find them is the day you'll join them."

~ ☾ ~

CHAPTER 5

Sloane stared at her third—or was it her fourth—drink as if Captain Morgan himself was going to step out of the glass with the advice she so desperately needed.

Her desire to do what was right overrode her desire for a sale.

That man rotting away back at that nursing home was a mass murderer. She knew it. And the only way to free the poor souls trapped in his house was to prove it. But she had no idea how to do that.

After her departure from Alvin's room, she drove through the early afternoon sunshine until she found a bar that was open. It was run-down, dirty, and smelled like the dark goo now sticking to her shoes so it reflected her mood quite nicely, and she decided it was as good a place as any for a drink—or five.

She tried to ignore the man that slid onto the bar stool next to her, focusing on her drink instead, but it was almost impossible to do. She could recognize those rugged good looks and wide shoulders anywhere. He smelled good too—like green grass on a summer day—and she found herself content to just sit beside him for a while, smelling.

Why wasn't she surprised he found her?

Jonah ordered a beer, then sat quietly, twirling the bottle in front of him. Sloane knew she shouldn't stare, it was just Jonah after all, but her gaze kept shifting from her suddenly boring glass to his beer. Why did she suddenly want to lean her head on his shoulder? To have him hold her?

~ ☾ ~

She shouldn't be having those thoughts.

Jonah had been Michael's best friend. She shouldn't ogle Michael's best friend.

Shoving those thoughts away as quickly as she could, she wondered if she was even drunk enough to contemplate those thing. It was one thing to imagine a man running his hand along your thigh when you were drunk, but entirely different when you were sober enough to know better.

From the way her head spun when she tried to turn it and how she couldn't feel the tip of her nose though she knew it was still attached to her face she decided she was probably drunk enough for the thoughts to surface, though she still reprimanded herself for thinking them. She focused on her glass again, bringing the sweet, spiced rum to her mouth for a sip.

"So," he paused, drawing out the word. "Why are we here?"

His voice was deep and husky. Sexy, like velvet on her skin. She closed her eyes for a moment, savoring the feel of it before taking a deep breath and turning to face him, taking note of his slightly mussed hair as she did.

"I'm mad." She told him as if that were an explanation.

"At your drink?" He took a sip of his beer, smiling at her from the side of his mouth.

"No. That's about the only thing I'm not mad at right now," she said.

"What happened?"

She grimaced, twirling her glass and watching the bubbles surface in the drink.

"How did you find me?" She turned on the stool to face him.

"I had Christa run your credit cards so I knew what your car looked like and you've been drinking here for over an hour. Plus she tracked your cell phone. You aren't hard to find."

~ ☾ ~

"You got here quick," she said.

"You're important to me."

"Don't lie to me, Jonah. It's the case. We both know it's the case so you don't have to pretend. I'll bet you're here because solving the twenty or so cold case files would look pretty good for your career."

"Why are you so mad?"

"Why am I mad?" She turned back to her glass, swirling the ice in the glass. "I'm mad because they're dead. All of them. And they're still suffering."

"There's nothing you can do about that, Sloane." He was trying to be sympathetic but she wanted none of it.

"You're right. There's nothing I can do about it. And therein lies the problem."

An uncomfortable silence stretched between them. Sloane wasn't used to being uncomfortable around Jonah and she didn't like it.

"What happened last night, Sloane?" His voice was soft. He always knew how to treat her. He knew what mattered and how to make things better. "What's really bothering you?"

He perched on his bar stool, his body turned away from her, but his eyes watched her intently.

"I don't really want to talk about it yet. I think I need to show you, not tell you about it."

She was silent for a moment. Did she want to go back there? Both yes and no. She knew she needed to because she was those girls only hope, but she also didn't want to.

"I'll get you coffee. Fancy flavored coffee we both know you spend the money on for yourself. Then we can stop by the hotel so I can check in and you can shower, maybe grab some Ibuprofen or something for that headache you're going to have and then we can get you some more coffee."

"I saw a local café down the street." She caved just as she knew she would.

~ ☾ ~

"Let's go." His stool scraped loudly on the floor as he pushed away from the bar. "I didn't fly to Wisconsin on a red eye so you could drink the day away. I have a feeling this is important."

And Jonah's *feelings* were nothing to be trifled with. If he had a feeling, she was going to trust him to solve this case.

Besides, he'd said the magic word.

Coffee.

Jonah drove her tiny rental car to the Mitchell house. It was strange having him squashed into the front seat with her. He dominated the space, smothering her with his rippling muscles and the scent of sandalwood and spice. It wasn't bad. It was just different.

.Cradling her coffee in her hands, she opened the window to try to let some of his static heat out. Sloane breathed in the cool air, letting it dance across her face and soothe her still pounding temples. He'd been right to remind her to grab some pain killers before they'd left. She had a pounding headache even her caramel latte couldn't beat.

"I'm sorry," Jonah said suddenly, breaking the silence as he slid the car into the driveway. "I'm frustrated and I shouldn't be taking it out on you."

"Why?" she asked.

"This house. This town. How this many women disappeared without the FBI becoming involved."

"And..." she prompted.

"And you saw Michael."

"I hoped to see him, but I didn't expect all these women."

"I know it's not your fault but that doesn't mean I can't worry about you." He reached over, placing his hand on her knee. For a second, she just stared at his large, sun bronzed fingers, feeling the heat of him seeping through her worn jeans.

~ ☾ ~

"I can take care of myself." Embarrassingly, her voice broke and her eyes grew warm and wet. She took a deep breath to steady herself. "It's not the first time I've been alone. I've adjusted to it again this past year. I'm better off by myself."

"I liked it better when you had Michael to take care of you."

"I did too, but that doesn't change anything," she said. "I'm not in danger. I have a few dozen spirits trying to save themselves."

Sloane was glad when he pulled into the driveway. She couldn't take another moment in the car. Slamming the door behind her, she stalked up the porch and used her key to open the door. Jonah followed close behind her.

It had been awhile since she seen him at work. She always was amazed by how sensitive he was to spirits. He could walk into a room and pick up on more than all of her equipment combined. If she was honest with herself, more than her lack of money or need to be alone, the reason she didn't have a partner for her business yet was because the one person she liked to work with was so devoted to the FBI she knew she would never be able to get him away from it. Nor would she want to. He was a born agent and she could never ask him to quit something he loved that much.

He stood in the center of Alvin's living room, his eyes scanning the open space.

"You said everything happened in the basement?" he asked.

"The first time I saw Michael was upstairs, but everything else has been in the basement."

"Michael isn't here. At least not right now." He shut his eyes, his voice quiet, as one of his hands reached out into the air. He pointed towards the kitchen. "Is that the direction of the basement? I feel the most energy there."

"Yes, the stairs are hidden in the back pantry."

~ ☾ ~

"Could you show me, please?"

She led him through the small kitchen area and down the stairs where his feet crunched on broken shards of glass from the night before.

Jonah didn't seem to notice. He paused for a moment, taking in the soiled recliner, all of the empty broken glasses she left on the floor and the incinerator before gloving up and turning back to her.

"Did you have a party here last night?" he asked.

She didn't answer. She couldn't joke about it yet and as he watched her, his smile faded and his tone turned serious.

"Sloane, tell me the truth. Are you all right?"

"What do you mean?" she hedged.

"I sense dozens of spirits here—none of them benevolent." He walked along the wall to avoid most of the glass, running his hand along the cement block. He stopped to open the incinerator door and glance inside. He bent down, wedged his flashlight in his mouth, and then scooted through the opening until only his feet stuck out.

"What are you doing?" She knelt next to him, trying to peer past his body. He held his small flashlight in his teeth as he used tweezers to pull something from the far corner of the unit.

"FBI secrets." His words were jumbled because of the flashlight but they still made her smile. "If I told you I'd have to kill you." He pushed himself out with a small plastic bag clutched in his hand.

"What is that?"

"Maybe nothing, but I'll take it to a local lab. I'm hoping it's a bit of a bone the lab can analyze. It was pretty clean in there though. Now stop changing the subject. What happened last night?"

"I did see ghosts last night. There were so many of them. I didn't know what to do. I went from never having contact before to being inundated with spirits in

~ ☾ ~

two nights. I panicked. It was more like they were warning me. They told me to leave and never come back."

His gaze tracked her as she paced the room. He didn't believe her. She could tell, but what else did he want her to say?

"All right, Sloane," he said. "Let's pretend for a moment that I'm not stupid. Why don't you try telling me the rest of the story? Otherwise, I can get right back on a flight to Washington and leave you here to deal with these murders."

"Michael helped me." She gave it to him straight. "I don't think the girls were trying to hurt me, just warn me, but whenever they touched me it burned. All they do is ask for water, like they're dying of thirst. I tried to bring them some, hence the broken glasses, but they couldn't drink it."

"Michael was a full body apparition," she continued. "He was like a bright light in full human form backlit in white." She tried to speak with clinical detachment but couldn't stop the tears.

She watched as he processed the information. In less than a moment he went from his brow furrowed in anger, to his eyes wide in astonishment and disbelief, before finally settling into the weary expression he tended to wear whenever she mentioned Michael.

"I know it sounds crazy," she continued before he responded. "But you, more than anyone else, should believe me. He knew us. He knew what we did. Why wouldn't he come back to contact us if he knew we'd listen? Besides, this job started on the year and a day anniversary of his death."

He crossed the room and folded her into his arms. For a moment, Sloane stiffened. She couldn't remember anyone hugging her since Michael's funeral. But as she inhaled Jonah's woodsy scent, she found herself relaxing her head into his chest.

~ ☾ ~

"I do believe you, Sloane," Jonah said. "I guess I'm just jealous though I have no right to be. He came to you. Not me. And I have to respect that."

"It was short-lived. You know how he always used to brighten up a room? It was like that. The other ghosts cowered from his light. And he spoke. He warned me and then he was gone again."

"But you're sure it was him?"

She nodded.

He opened his mouth as if he were about to say more, but nothing came out. Instead, he released her, dropping his arms to his sides. Sloane felt cold and suddenly bereft without his warmth around her. Reaching up, she placed her hand on his cheek.

"He loved you too," she said quietly.

He turned his face into her hand, his lips brushing softly against her palm.

"I know he did. He just loved you more." He smiled sadly.

With a sigh, he stepped away from her, going to the far wall of the basement where Karen's picture hung on the wall. Wiping off the dusty picture, he removed it from its hook for a closer look.

"Hello Karen Hartwell?" he said.

"How do you know about Karen Hartwell?" Sloane asked.

"It's my job to know, Sloane. I deal with cold case files in the continental U.S. and that's what you've uncovered here."

"Alvin told me how love never worked out for them." Sloane said. "I think she was the first to die and he kept her picture as a reminder." She followed him over, straightening the picture and studying the girl's face.

"He may have known her, but I don't know about the rest of them. My question is how our murderer got them into the house and down here. Drugged their drinks? But why would someone drink with an old man? Maybe

~ ☾ ~

he overpowered them or tricked them into helping him
or something."

"Can you feel them?" Sloane asked.

He rested his hand against the wall, closing his eyes.
"I can sense them but they aren't active right now. It
would be better for me if it was night but I only sense
their fear. And pain. Lots of pain."

Sloane stayed quiet, letting him work.

"And they're angry because they're still trapped.
They're thirsty. So thirsty. All they want is a drink but
they're trapped. And nothing will quench their thirst any
longer."

"Last night they kept asking for water. Demanding it
really." She shuddered, remembering the sunken faces
and bony fingers reaching for her.

He glanced at her as if he'd forgotten she was there
for a second. Sloane tried not to be insulted. She knew
how he worked. He immersed himself in the case, but it
was her mystery to solve after all.

"What do you think of him?" There was concern in his
tone.

"He makes my skin crawl, but he's dying. He can't do
anything from a nursing home."

Sloane wandered the room, methodically stacking the
few unbroken water glasses strewn about the floor.

"But you think he is a murderer?" Jonah asked.

"I think he could be," she said.

"I'd like to meet him," Jonah said.

Sloane sighed, using the recliner to pull herself up.
She needed a broom to get rid of all of this glass.

"Help me clean up and I'll take you there."

Alvin was staring out a small window at a small patch
of grass visible from his room when the nurse let Sloane
into the room. He turned, a small smile playing across
his lips until Jonah stepped in behind her.

"Back again, and with a bodyguard this time? I

~ ☾ ~

wouldn't think you would acknowledge the need for protection around me."

"I wouldn't even acknowledge you were human if I wasn't forced to."

His wide smile was cunning as if he knew something she didn't.

She felt the warmth of Jonah's arm as he wrapped it around her waist, pulling her back against him. For a moment it felt so right to have his arm around her, she almost leaned into him.

"Back off," he breathed into her ear so only she could hear. "Remember that things aren't always what they seem. Besides, maybe I like being thought of as your bodyguard."

Wagging his eyebrows comically, he stepped past her, coming fully into the room and placing himself between her and Alvin. Sloane could barely see the old man around the hulk of Jonah's body, but she relished in the change in him as he was confronted by a man bigger than he'd ever been in his life. Leaning against the wall, she watched Jonah in action.

"Alvin," Jonah said. "I'm Special Agent Prescott of the FBI." He pulled a black wallet out of the breast pocket of his jacket, flashing his badge in front of Alvin's face. "I'm researching some cold case files in the area. Twenty-six to be precise."

"That's nice," Alvin pushed himself into a sitting position. "But what does it have to do with me?"

"Could be nothing," Jonah ran his hand over the dark stubble covering his chin as he sat on the edge of Alvin's bed. "I was informed by Miss Osborne here, that there is something peculiar about your house and I can only wonder if the two might be combined?"

"You can only wonder? And here I was worried that you might know something." He wheezed a laugh, glancing at Sloane as if she would find him funny too. Sloane glared at him, and his smile fell. His voice

~ ☾ ~

wasn't as confident when he continued. "Not that I've done anything except get old. I'm an old man dying of lung cancer. Have you two found something in my house?"

"Why? Is there something in your house we should find?" asked Jonah.

"Well, you're the FBI. You flashed me your badge like you're better than the rest of us. It's not my job to do yours, Special Agent Prescott."

Jonah ignored the comment, focusing on the job instead. "How would you explain the presence of so many spirits in your house?"

"It's my magnetic personality. Females have always been attracted to me." Alvin leered at Sloane, running his tongue slowly over his lips. "Even your girl here. She can't stop looking at me."

Sloane tasted bile in her throat but didn't give Alvin the pleasure of seeing her react in any way. In front of her, she saw the muscles in Jonah's back tense and knew he was mad.

"Well, let's talk about your way with women then?" Jonah said, his voice sharp. "Let's talk about Karen Hartwell. You remember Karen, don't you?"

"Of course I remember Karen," Alvin turned his attention back to Jonah. "She was my first love."

"That may be, but from what I've heard, she did not love you." Jonah reached into his bag and drew out a file from the small briefcase he carried with him. "This is her old case file, because she, unlike the rest of the girls, did catch the attention of the FBI. Her case in unsolved. Although you had a firm alibi for the night, babysitting your nephew or something, but you were mentioned several times by her friends and family."

"Of course I would be mentioned. We had been dating." Alvin said.

"There's nothing in here about a relationship," Jonah opened the file, flipping the pages until he found what

~ ☾ ~

he needed. "Actually, you're described as obsessive. A stalker."

"Then your reports are inaccurate." Sloane had never seen Alvin look more serious. "She loved me. It might have taken her awhile to admit it but, in the end, even she knew the truth."

"How can you be so sure?" Jonah asked.

"She told me." Alvin said.

"And what about these other girls?" Jonah flipped to the back of the file where he'd handwritten a list of names. "Jessica Boyd, Meredith McDermont, Sarah Miller. I could go on. Do any of those names ring a bell?"

Alvin rested his chin in his hands, appearing to ponder the names. A small smile played across his face as his eyes lit up.

"Miller. I think I remember that name. Wasn't she in that movie about a chainsaw murderer that came out a few years ago?"

Jonah glanced at his notes again.

"Sarah Miller lived in Milwaukee. She disappeared about three years ago."

Alvin laughed, his whole body shaking though his dark eyes remained focused on Jonah.

"Three years ago? Why would I remember what I was doing three years ago? Do you want me to just admit it? Would that make your plush little desk job easier so you could file your papers in tidy order?" Alvin faked a pout, his eyes on Jonah. His voice turned sing-song as he mocked the case. "Well, mister FBI man, I guess you caught me. I remember that three years ago today I chopped up a girl and put her in my incinerator and watched her burn. Is that what you wanted to hear?"

Sloane watched Jonah's fist clench and unclench at his side. It was the only sign of the anger she knew he was working to contain. She had to get him out of the room before he exploded.

~ ☾ ~

CHAPTER 6

"Jonah..."

"Yes, Sloane?" He shifted his weight but didn't turn his body around to meet her gaze. He never looked away from the old man.

Crazy old Alvin's stare was fixated on her. A chilling smile played at on the corners of his lips as though he'd hidden aces up each sleeve. His eyes held no emotion. Was he a madman who could've ripped her throat out and drank her blood if he had the strength? She began to mentally simmer as if anger could make her boil like water on the stove. Enough of Alvin's games.

"Can I please talk to you outside Jonah?" She didn't wait for his response before she left the room. *Alvin gets bathed? Food brought to him?* These simple luxuries of a nursing home infuriated her!

Jonah joined her, the white florescent lights of the hallway making him squint.

"That man in there is a psychopath," she seethed, pacing the hallway. "We need to prove it before God himself avenges the old geezer and his lungs fill up with blood and he drowns or something."

"Nice visual. And I couldn't agree more," Jonah was the epitome of calm, cool, and collected.

"Argh!" She balled her fists, but there was nothing around to punch.

"Sugar melts, shit floats, and he'll get what he deserves. Michelangelo said 'Genius is eternal patience.' So let's be smart. Don't let him see he's getting to you. That fuels him."

~ ☾ ~

"You shut off being pissed at a killer and somehow replace it with logic and truth. How the hell do you do that?" she wondered.

"It's an instinct for survival and takes years of practice. So there's no hope for you." He rustled her hair.

"You're only tough on the outside."

His face softened. "I'm only tough because I have to be. Heart off, head on. I'd tell you to try it, but it's lonely. And I like you just how you are. It's cute."

"Cute?" She was tempted to stomp her foot like a three-year old. He was right of course.

Her heart overpowered her logical head in almost every situation. And that had gotten her in more trouble than she cared to recall. "Fine. What's your plan? I assume you have one?"

Jonah popped some gum in his mouth from his pocket and checked his cell—all business. "Let's let Alvin sit for now. He's not going anywhere. I want to talk to his sheriff neighbor. Maybe he's seen or heard something around that house." He zipped his jacket and took three steps down the hall before he turned. "Coming?"

Sloane took one last peek into Alvin's room. He brightened, wheeling himself toward the door. He held one hand to the side of his mouth like he was telling her some great secret. "You don't need his help, Ms. Osborne." He paused to cough up more phlegm into his blood-soaked handkerchief. "I'm sure this is a job you can handle all by your lonesome."

The old-fashioned diner in the center of town was still packed even though it was hours past lunch. Sloane slid into the booth across from Jonah grimacing when her leg stuck to the duct tape patching the ripped red pleather seats. A mousy pot-bellied twenty-something with a taught apron and thick eyeliner emerged from

~ ☾ ~

behind the bar with two battered menus. Popping her gum, she meandered through the tables before wiping off theirs and collecting the tip left by the previous customers. She waited, chomping on her gum and checking her reflection in the window as they perused the menu.

Since the sheriff couldn't see them at the station until after lunch, Jonah had suggested they get a bite to eat. The only two options on the town square were a hoity coffee shop with ten dollar sandwiches and lattes or the local diner where she eaten yesterday. On her budget, the diner would suffice.

"What can I get you?" The gum-popping waitress directed her question at Jonah.

Sloane longed for yesterday's waitress immediately.

"How about coffee and the farmer's skillet with extra cheese darling? I'm a breakfast for dinner kind of guy." Jonah winked at the waitress, shut his menu and handed it to her with a flourish. Then he went back to his digital life of emails.

A flush brightened her cheeks. "I'll have that right up for you, sir." But she didn't budge.

"Ahem." Sloane cleared her throat several times.

The waitress stood transfixed, ogling Jonah like a deer in headlights. He didn't seem to notice so she yanked his cell out of his hand.

"Can you please tell her I'd like the same as you, no mushrooms." Sloane enunciated.

"Oh, sorry." The waitress scribbled Sloane's order on her notepad and hurried to the kitchen.

"Do you have to hit on everyone? It's embarrassing." She sighed.

"Just trying to improve the life of every woman I meet. Ya know, civic duty and all." He reached his hand out to get his cell back.

Sloane rolled her eyes.

"What?" he shrugged, "Every woman has something

~ ☾ ~

beautiful about them. I just like to remind them what it is. So, that's not flirting. Besides, you should always be more than polite to people who handle your food. That's my policy."

After the waitress filled their mugs with liquid warmth and they sugar and creamed their coffee to glorious—albeit not Starbuck's level—perfection, Sloane took her first sip of deliciousness. Time to get down to business. "So what's really going on with you?"

"What are you talking about?" He sipped his coffee.

"You're more checked out than usual. Why?"

"You know why. I'm working a case."

"Jonah, it's me. I probably know you better than anyone. You fly here after one phone call now you're acting like it's all business?"

He chewed his lip and he reached across to a recently vacated table and snatched the sports section, unfurling it to hide himself from view. "Gotta love those Packers. Did you know there're like eight-hundred Green Bay Packer bars in this country?"

She pushed the paper down. "Fascinating tidbit. Now talk to me."

"We are talking."

She sipped her coffee. Should she say it? "Why did you come all the way here? Miss me or something?"

Then for about five seconds, the Jonah she remembered, was there. His rich, brown eyes softened his eyes and his walls crumpled like the newspaper on the table. His gaze penetrated straight through her and caused her body to hum in a way she never felt before. Like they weren't in a diner in Wisconsin. Time and space froze with his undivided attention. All she once, she got twitchy and uncomfortable. Had Michael ever made her feel like this?

She knew the answer and the truth of it gnawed at her.

He grasped her hands across the table. She interlaced

~ ☾ ~

her fingers with his and felt the pulse of energy pass between them. "Sloane, we...I...God, I miss you. All the time. I know why you're doing this and I understand but that doesn't mean I'm happy about it. And I can feel when you're in trouble. I felt you needed me so strong last night that I dropped everything and caught the first flight here. You're in danger. I can feel it all around you." Releasing her hands, he laughed. "I know that sounds crazy, but whatever..."

Sloane said nothing at first. "It's not crazy. I can feel—" His cell rang, interrupting her. Why did he smile at his caller ID? She wanted to finish her sentence.

"Hey partner in crime, whatcha got for me?"

All her emotions died when he answered the phone playfully. She slumped in the booth and her mood turned black. Was she jealous of his partner? But she couldn't be jealous because it was Jonah. She didn't have any right to him. And she didn't want to. Did she?

Jonah covered the receiver and mouthed to Sloane, "I have to take this. It's Christa."

Sloane was saved from responding when a steaming omelet was placed before her, giving

her something to do besides pout. Jonah's partner, Agent Christa McBride was no one Sloane could compete with. They'd met briefly at Michael's funeral and now Sloane had to swallow the bile that rose in her throat any time she was mentioned.

Agent McBride was thin yet muscular and gorgeously blonde. She should have waited for him in the car at the funeral instead of intruding on a private affair. But instead, she hovered behind him, offering moral support. Patronizing bitch had actually said, "I'm so sorry for your loss Sloane. But Jonah, are you ready to go?"

When Sloane had made her thoughts known to him, Jonah laughed. Did her breasts jiggle perfectly when they ran their seven minute miles together on Saturday

~ ☾ ~

mornings? That damn woman gobbled up all his time.

Yep, time to admit it. Sloane was definitely jealous.

Jonah's eyes scanned the diner. "Really? Uh-huh." Pause. "Yeah, Sloane says 'hi' too."

Sloane shook her head and ran her index finger across her throat to which Jonah winked at her. He didn't hang up so Sloane tried another tactic. She poked him in the arm to get his attention. "Ask her 'What do you call twenty blondes in a freezer?'"

Jonah cocked his head.

"Frosted flakes."

Smirking, he turned back to his conversation. "Oh yeah? How did you find that out?"

Sloane strained to hear what Miss Bubbly voice was saying. Probably something about some cool FBI case. Then she heard Christa mention her name...

She was working on this case too?

"I can't leave. You go."

Sloane consoled herself in knowing that the young detective couldn't possibly know the real Jonah like she did. Sloane was sure no one had her level of intimacy with Jonah. Wait, his personal life was none of her business!

When he clicked the phone shut, he was one-hundred percent checked out again and back in work mode, complete with furrowed eyebrows and fingers tapping on the table.

She knew why. Because to *feel*, to actually let yourself be present in the moment and *feel*, meant life could throw pain at you from every direction in a heartbeat. Better to be checked out and have walls around your heart to protect yourself. Jonah had a job that wouldn't allow him to get close to anyone. He did what he did out of self-preservation but she hated it all the same.

"So what's up and why did she mention my name?"

"Tip called into the FBI on the cold case regarding Karen Hartwell. The informant will only deliver the

~ ☾ ~

information in person to me. In D.C. I'd have to fly back today, but I can't leave you," Jonah said.

"Yes you can. If Alvin told someone you're here and they're willing to talk, you have to go. You can't risk them withholding the information if Agent Boobalicious shows up instead. I'll be fine." Sloane hoped that was the truth.

"Boobalicious," he laughed. "Ok, but promise me you won't go back in that house alone."

Shrugging her noncommittal shoulders, Sloane added, "I'll talk to the sheriff."

At the cop shop, Sloane reread the questions Jonah had jotted down for her. She was back in charge of the investigation. After announcing herself through the bullet-proof window, she now waited to see the sheriff on a stiff backed chair.

She prided herself on being fiercely independent, yet having Jonah by her side would sure have improved the atmosphere. He'd left her with a stern "Be careful" and brotherly pat on the shoulder saying he'd call from D.C. after meeting with the informant. How insulting. He even scribbled a list of questions for her to ask the sheriff. Wasn't this her show? She smoothed her hair and had put on the only button-up shirt she owned. Time to take charge of *her* investigation.

The sheriff strolled into the station fifteen minutes late with coffee in one hand and the same Sports section Jonah had been trying to read in the other.

"I guess you didn't need my help last night, Miss Osborne." He folded the paper in half and placed it in a metal trashcan. His six-sided Star of David badge shone on his chest when he strode past her. Sloane hurried along behind him into the bowels of the precinct. The nametag on the office door read "Sheriff Glen Spencer".

She halted in the doorway leaning against the door frame, finally putting it together. "You're G. Spencer?

~ (~

You're the person trying to buy Alvin's house? Why didn't you just tell me that?"

"I should have told you, but I didn't want to interfere with your investigation. I hired you for my wife, Lily." He motioned to a five by seven wedding portrait on his desk. A decorative silver frame held a much younger version of Glen with a primly dressed woman holding a small bouquet standing under a wooden crucifix. His grey eyes glazed over and he rubbed his thumb over the picture. "Lily always wanted to buy that house, rip it down and extend her flower garden. She loved gardening."

"Why hire me?"

The sheriff coughed and tried to appear more formal. "I told you this story when we first met. Lily wanted her garden but didn't want to upset any spirits. My Lily has been gone for a while. Alvin's house spooked her. Always did. She thought it needed an exorcism or something. Before she left, she made me promise to either move, or to see if the place was haunted and give the spirits peace. Is that something you can do for me Miss Osborne? I really don't want to move and now that the house has been vacant for so long, I just couldn't ignore Lily's wishes any longer. I'm sorry, I know I sound like a fool...but last night. Tell me. Lily was right?"

"I'm afraid so. Why didn't you introduce yourself to me right away?" she asked.

"I didn't come clean on who I was 'cause if word gets out around here, people will think I'm nuts." His hands sat peacefully on his large desk calendar and he twiddled his thumbs. "To tell you the God's honest truth, Alvin Mitchell has always given me the creeps. The only reason I'm interested is the location. So, does the place need a spiritual cleansing?"

Not so much as a piece of paper was out of place in his office. Everything was labeled, organized, or stacked.

~ ☾ ~

His walls were dotted with awards, certificates, and pictures of him shaking hands with people. With Jonah jetting off to D.C., Sloane figured this might be the right time to get the authorities involved, especially since he was buying the house anyway.

"What do you know about Alvin and his connection with the missing women in this town?" Sloane watched for any reaction—a sigh or a hand his head, anything— but all the sheriff did was stare right at her.

"Alvin is a frail old man. What would he have to do with the missing girls in this town?" Glen cracked his neck. "But it's true we have too many cold case files. After Lily...well, it was sometimes too hard for me to look at these cases and I have to admit, that because we're right on the railroad tracks, I always assumed they were runaways or that vagrants snatched them and hopped cargo trains with them. There is only me and no support staff to look into these disappearances." He stood and pointed a stack of dusty files in the corner.

"Did Alvin ever mention a woman named Karen Hartwell to you?"

The sheriff shook his head. "No, but I've seen her file. It's from twenty some years ago. I wasn't even on the force then. Moved into my house about fifteen years ago. Alvin and I have never been on the best of terms. We only talked when I told him to clean up his yard or bring in his garbage cans. Guy was a loner asshole if you ask me. Why? Did he mention Karen?"

Sloane produced her file on the house from a crisp manila envelope. The history she collected on the town, notes she written in the late night hours after talking with Alvin, and the evidence on the haunting she collected thus far. "That house is haunted all right. I have reason to believe women were held, tortured, and murdered there. It's going to need more than, as you called it...a spiritual cleansing. And now the FBI may become involved. I think Alvin's first victim may have

~ ☾ ~

been Karen Hartwell. Can I take a look at those cold case files?"

The sheriff took a blank white piece of paper from his top drawer and a freshly sharpened pencil from his desk. He wrote the name in capital letters. "I will look at that file right away, but are you sure bumps in the night from your ultrasensitive equipment makes old man Mitchell the prime suspect in thirty years of missing women?" He smiled with coffee-stained teeth. "But best never to leave a stone unturned. Oh course you can look at those files. I'll keep Karen's for a little while until I can look it over and talk to Alvin. Did you say something about the FBI? I have to say, I'd actually appreciate the help."

Sloane stood up to leave. "For right now, Sheriff, I can't in good conscious recommend you complete the purchase. The spirits there need to be put to rest, and the only way to do that is to catch their murderer."

He leaned forward, his elbows on the desk. Steepling his fingers in front of his face he watched her above his hands. "I don't believe in ghosts myself but, since you're the expert, I'll trust your judgment. I'm on board and if you need any help with your investigation, please know you have the full support of me and my department."

"I appreciate that." She shook his hand with her free one. "I want you to know that not only do I verify that a house is haunted, but I ensure for the new owner that it's a safe environment to live in. If a ghost is hostile, I recommend exorcism or a cleansing instead of keeping it haunted. You can't rip the house down anytime soon, as that would trap the ghosts forever. We need to find out for sure what happened there first." She turned to leave. "Good day, Sheriff."

Even after an afternoon nap in her cheap motel room, saying her mood was pissy was an understatement. She punched Jonah's number in her phone from her perch in Alvin's ratty recliner in the basement.

~ ☾ ~

"Hey," she said, remembering his brotherly pat.

"Hey. Guess what?" he said.

"What?"

"No one showed. I'm on my way back." Even Jonah sounded surprised.

"No shit? Well get this. Glen the sheriff is my real client. He wants the bad juju out of the house so he can rip it down and build a garden for his dead wife that was convinced the place was haunted!"

She heard Jonah swear under his breath. "Sit tight until I get back to you. Okay?"

"Okay." She snapped the phone shut and set it down. Before Jonah returned to the investigation, she tried to make contact with Michael one more time. Last night, he'd *spoken* to her. Actual words that reached her ears.

She closed her eyes and let herself see him again. The real Michael. The Michael that clipped lilacs and arranged them perfectly for her birthday last year, the Michael who brushed her hair when she was stressed, and the Michael that would have been the perfect husband after she had worn the perfect dress and had the perfect wedding.

Sucks life ain't perfect.

The hours ticked by and no knocking, no ghosts pouring out of the walls, and no Michael.

Circling the basement, she examined every inch of the place once again. What was she missing? Cement floor and cinder block walls, the incinerator, the lounge chair. Nothing new. Nothing unusual. Nothing...

Plopping back down in the recliner, she reached down and pulled the level to raise her feet. It slide upward with ease and she hear a click but her feet were still planted on the floor. What the heck? It probably needed to be pulled away from the wall. With a heave, she yanked the chair but noticed something out of the corner of her eye.

Behind the chair by Karen's picture, the wall had

~ ☾ ~

shifted...open! The lever was a trigger to a secret lock that revealed a false wall. Her heart thumped in her throat as her fingers wrapped around one of the false cinder blocks. She heaved open the door and peered inside. A long dark hallway filled with one thing. Utter darkness.

Without warning, something pushed her hard from the back. She tripped forward and heard the wall slam shut behind her.

She was trapped.

~ ☾ ~

CHAPTER 7

The dark surrounded her, cloaking her in blackness. Sloane couldn't see anything in front of her, but she could feel the weight of the walls around her. She turned back, pushing against the solid wall where the door had just been, but nothing moved. She was trapped.

Heart hammering in her chest, she leaned back against the wall, forcing herself to take deep breaths; in through the nose, out through the mouth. Calm.

"Don't panic, Sloane," she said aloud. "You've been in worse situations than this before."

But she hadn't, and she knew it.

The darkness was a powerful shroud, cloaking her so she was blind. Even after a moment to allow her eyes to adjust to the black, she still couldn't see her hand in front of her face. Nothing penetrated the dark fog except the sound of the steady drip she also heard from Alvin's basement. It was louder now, and thumped like a drumbeat, echoing into the darkness around her.

Using her hands as a guide, she found she was in a tunnel. It wasn't large, she could reach both sides without stretching her arms to full length, and the ceiling was just above her head. The surface was cool to the touch and smooth, like stone. With her fingertips she could just make out the rectangular blocks like the ones lining the basement. Ahead of her was the still empty air of a tunnel. It smelled stale and musty, like the air had been trapped down here for years and Sloane hoped she wouldn't suffer the same fate.

Having no other choice, Sloane stretched her arms in

~ ☾ ~

front of her and felt her way down the passageway. Careful of each step, she took her time sliding each foot along the floor until she was sure there were no obstacles she couldn't see in the darkness. Her brain conjured images of the bodies of the women who were now ghosts lining the hall, but as she moved forward, she encountered nothing but empty space.

She continued her slow progress until she sensed a wall in front of her. Her heart stumbled in her chest as she felt the wall, searching for any exit. Gasping short, hysterical breaths, she felt tears burning in her eyes and her panic mounting. She stumbled to the left and realized the tunnel made an abrupt turn and didn't end.

Sloane stopped and she laughed at her own hysterics, the harsh sound echoing down the hall.

The passageway turned again after about twenty feet, this time to the right, and down that tunnel there was a grayness that could only mean light.

Moving faster now, Sloane moved towards the lessening of darkness like it were a beacon of hope. She prayed like she never prayed before, asking God for an exit. A door. A hole. Anything that would help her escape.

What she didn't expect was to find the source of the light was a young woman crouched in a corner, facing the wall as though being punished.

The woman looked about thirty with dark brown hair, a tangled mess of curls cocooning around her emaciated frame. A shapeless shell shirt that might have been a bright green now darkened and stained from wear, hung around her form, baring a thin shoulder. Snug black pants clung to her thighs, while dirty pink legwarmers covered her calves above what was left of white Keds sneakers. She reminded Sloane of an older version of the girl from Flashdance, except her entire body gave off enough of a glow to dimly light the passage and she was transparent. Sloane could make out every crack in the cement blocks in the wall behind her.

~ ☾ ~

Sloane caught her breath, stopping in her tracks as she watched the woman. It was a full body manifestation. Without any equipment or prep, this woman was appearing before her. It was astonishing.

The woman held out her hand to catch a drop of water as it fell from a crack in the ceiling. The water passed right through her palm, splattering on the damp floor.

"Hello?" Sloane's voice was tentative, even to her own ears. It was one thing to talk to Michael, but he was a ghost she known in life. It was another to start a conversation with a dead stranger. "Can you hear me?"

The woman didn't turn, her whole body focused on the next drop of water until it had floated through her hand again.

The woman sighed, sitting back on her heels as she watched the wall.

"Water," she rasped. "Do you have any water?"

"I'm sorry. I don't have anything." Sloane said. "I tried to give you water last night, but no one drank it."

"What are you doing here? You aren't supposed to be here!" The woman's voice was so raspy Sloane could barely hear her. She turned her head slowly as though removing her gaze from the little bit of water seeping through the stone was painful. When her gaze finally rested on Sloane, her eyes were dark black pits, swirling with tiny dancing lights.

Sloane stepped back involuntarily, then gathered her courage to approach the apparition. She could sense the poor girl wasn't dangerous. She was trapped here as much as Sloane was herself.

"I found the secret door and got pushed in." Sloane said. "Then the door shut behind me and I couldn't get out."

"Ah, you must have been at Alvin's house," the woman rose to her feet. "Not a safe place to be. Though nothing about this area is safe."

~ ☾ ~

"You knew Alvin?" Sloane asked.

The look the woman gave Sloane was laughable. "Do you think I'd be down here if I hadn't? I knew him better than anyone. That's why I was never in the hole. Doesn't make much difference, hole or tunnel. You still die."

"What do you mean you knew Alvin better than anyone?" Sloane asked.

"Alvin's my brother."

"No way." Sloane slumped against the wall, staring at the apparition. Lily began to flicker slightly as if she were fading. "Your own brother killed you?"

The ghost cocked her head, looking at Sloane with those eerie eyes making Sloane shiver and step away from the ghost again.

"My brother loved me. He would not have killed me."

"So you're telling me Alvin is not a murderer?" Sloane cocked an eye in disbelief, leaning against the wall and folding her arms across her chest. There was no way this woman could convince her that crazy Alvin was not a murderer.

The spirit laughed without warmth, her whole body flickering in and out of sight as her shoulders rocked.

"Oh, no. I would never try to convince you of that. Alvin murdered poor Karen Hartwell. Everyone knows that. But he didn't murder me."

"What are you talking about?" Sloane asked. "Who was your husband?"

"When Alvin came back from the working construction in Chicago he was different. Quiet. And he'd brought his handsome friend with him. I loved him immediately. That was my big mistake. Everything my husband did was calculated and planned, even our marriage. He's still planning now. You know that, don't you?"

"Know what?" Sloane asked.

"That you're the next victim. He wants you to join us in our pain."

~ ☾ ~

The ghost flickered and her light went out leaving Sloane in complete darkness again. She sighed heavily, missing the girl's light more than the conversation before continuing down the passageway. She had to find an exit.

Sloane followed a sliver of light in the tunnel and came to a reinforced steel door that was left ajar. The light came from a small wire lamp resting on a metal desk. It barely illuminated the desktop but was enough to hearten her.

The desk was devoid of paper but had an extensive array of computer and recording apparatus. Sloane flipped open the laptop and let it buzz to life while she examined the rest of the equipment. It was standard video recording tools, along with some black light and what looked like the night vision goggles she seen special ops guys wear in the movies.

When the computer powered up, Sloane looked down at the screen. She could barely make out the picture but it seemed to be the view from a camera pointing into the darkness. Her heart thumped in her chest. What was going on here?

Slipping the night-vision goggles over her head, she turned them on and scanned the dark room. There weren't any windows but large vents along the ceiling allowing air to flow and a steel door at the far end. Sloane picked her way slowly across the room until she came to the door. It was locked, but then she expected it to be.

She turned, ignoring the flare from the single lamp as she scanned the rest of the room and saw a perfectly circular hole dug into the floor. Approaching it carefully, Sloane perched at the side of the hole to look down. It was at least fifteen feet down.

A light switched on in the room, painfully blinding her in the goggles. She screamed at the painful light,

~ ☾ ~

wrenching the mask from her face and tossing it to the side as she closed her eyes against the brightness.

"Welcome, Sloane." A man's voice whispered behind her.

She jerked upright when strong arms lifted her about the waist. She fought, scratching at the exposed skin on his arm and kicking with all her might, but the man tossed her easily into the hole. She managed to save her head and land awkwardly on one shoulder, rolling into a somersault that only propelled her into one of the hole's walls.

She struggled to her feet, balling her hands into tight fists and rising on her toes to be ready for the next attack. Instead she heard mocking laughter above her. Looking up, she saw the silhouette of a man at the edge of the hole.

For some reason, Sloane didn't feel fear. Instead anger pulsed from her, giving her strength.

She lunged for the man, trying to reach the side and pull herself up, but the hole was too deep. She was trapped but that didn't stop her from trying to scale the walls until she had to stop, leaning over, hands on her knees, panting.

"Oh, I was right to bring you here. I knew I was." The man's voice sounded familiar but her panicked brain couldn't place it.

"Bring me here? What are you talking about?" she asked.

"You're going to be the best entertainment I've had in years."

She was going to escape. And then she was going to kill whoever this bastard was who'd shoved her in this hole.

"Who are you?" Sloane screamed. "Why are you doing this?"

"Just calm down, Sloane. A girl needs to know when she's beaten."

~ ☾ ~

"You'll never beat me," she spat.

"I can see you need your first lesson in obedience." The man walked away from the hole to where Sloane couldn't see him anymore. "Remember, you asked for this. It is your fault, not mine."

When she heard the hissing of gas being pumped into the hole, she didn't fight it. What was the point? She couldn't hold her breath forever. Instead she succumbed to the inevitable, wondering if she'd ever wake again.

Sloane woke with her cheek pasted to a cool cement floor. Something was very wrong. She wasn't sleeping in her lumpy hotel bed. For a moment she thought she fallen asleep in the basement of Alvin's house, then she remembered the false door and the corridor through the darkness.

She sat up, rubbing her pounding temples as she tried to remember. It was hard to think past a headache that made her want to vomit.

She'd been shoved in a pit. That's right. Gassed by some sick bastard who hadn't even identified himself.

There was some light now. Enough she could look around for any hope of escape. All she could see was gray. Gray floor. Gray walls. Gray ceiling far above her. The pit was a deep hole made of smoothly poured concrete that left no space for hand or footholds. All around her was just smooth circular walls rising at least fifteen feet into the air.

Faint light came from a small lantern hung on a rope above the opening. A tiny camera was suspended next to the lantern, obviously so they wouldn't miss any of the action in the pit. Probably an infrared camera, so it could see her in the dark.

When she was able to lift her head a bit farther, she was rewarded by the sight of Alvin Mitchell sitting awkwardly in a frayed blue and black folding chair, oxygen at his side, the tubes running from the tank to

~ ☾ ~

his nose. He rasped each breath as he leaned forward to see her. Comfortable in a chair at the edge of the hole, an oxygen tank at his side.

"I see Sleeping Beauty is finally awake." The old man produced a hearty chuckle that quickly turned into a wheezing cough.

"Are you trying to be funny, Alvin? Because you're not."

Sloane heart was hammering in her chest and she could feel the heat rising through her. She wanted to sit down and cry. How had she let this happen? She should have listened to Jonah and stayed home, but she wanted to see Michael again and look where that had gotten her. She crossed her arms over her chest, trying to keep Alvin from noticing her hands were shaking. Mustering as much bravado as she could manage, she glared up at him as though she wasn't trapped in a hole in his basement but was sitting across the table from him at a private party.

"Just stating the obvious."

She got to him. His smile disappeared and his brows drew together in concern.

"You're amazing." Sloane pulled herself to her feet. "I thought you were dying and, yet, here you are."

Her stomach rumbled with hunger though she ignored it, smacking her dry lips as she tried to bring the fluid to her mouth. It felt like she'd been chewing on cotton balls in her sleep.

"I am dying." Alvin coughed into his handkerchief and Sloane leaned back against her prison wall while she waited for him to finish. "I'm dying." He repeated as he put the handkerchief back into his front shirt pocket. "I'm on a family outing. The nurses never deny me anything."

"You have more than just a sister?" she asked.

"How do you know about my sister?" he demanded.

She cocked her head to the side, watching him as he scrutinized her.

~ ☾ ~

"Did you get a city permit to build this torture chamber?" She pushed off the wall, swinging herself in a circle so just the tips of her middle fingers brushed along the walls. "I bet the inspector would have had a field day with this one. Or did you just pay a local guy cash? Enough to keep him quiet?"

"How do you know the building inspector wasn't a woman and she's down there with you right now in spirit?" Alvin's smile was starting to annoy her.

"I know Karen was an accident. You didn't mean to kill her. And the rest of the girls weren't your fault either. For some reason I cannot even begin to fathom, your sister still loves and believes in you. Can you explain that to me?"

He stared at her until Sloane had to lower her eyes. There was too much turmoil in the depths of his cold blue eyes. He was in pain, more pain than she could even imagine and not just from his disease.

"I can't explain that." His voice was softer, like he was giving her information he shouldn't. "I don't want to talk about her. But my brother-in-law was in the concrete business. The hole was his idea."

"Sounds like he's the crazy one in this operation, and that's saying a lot," Sloane muttered but Alvin laughed.

"I admired your spunk from the first. That's why I finally agreed to add you to the collection."

Collection.

To him that's what they all were. A collection. That's what *she* was now.

Sloane glanced away from him, trying to hide her revulsion. She wondered what parts he collected, because it had to be something. A bit of hair. A tooth. Something to remember them by.

"He thought you'd make a great finale for me." Alvin added.

Sloane was so immersed in her own panic – the bile filling her throat with its tangy acid threatening to spill

~ ☾ ~

over – she almost missed this last comment. Fighting against her body's reaction, Sloane tried to concentrate.

Who was *HE*?

This brother-in-law?

She was missing something.

Something important.

"What are you telling her, you stupid old man?" another voice said.

Another man was in the room. Sloane couldn't see him, but she knew that voice. It was the man who'd dumped her in the hole the night before.

Alvin shrunk into himself. The cool self-importance he always oozed disappeared and he became the hollow old man he really was.

"Get away from the pit, asshole." The voice said. "I never told you to talk to her. I told you to let me know when she woke up."

"I'm sorry. I know I should have called. She tricked me into talking to her."

"Yeah, I'm sure. Probably smiled at you and your cock responded. You're a disgusting old man. Remember that. I should have left you in the home. I don't need you for this anymore. It's out of sheer kindness I've included you this time."

"Yes, Glen. You're right, of course. Thank you for including me."

Sloane's jaw dropped and she knew her eyes were as big as saucers.

Glen!

Did he just say Glen?

As in Glen the sheriff? Glen the buyer for the house?

She was in more trouble than she thought.

"Go back over to the monitors," Glen told Alvin. "Monitor something. Make sure no one is snooping around. I want to talk to Sloane."

There were a few moments of shifting while Alvin pulled his oxygen container away from the pit. Then

~ ☾ ~

Glen sat in the lawn chair, resting one foot on the side of the pit so the dirty soles of his shoes hung over the edge. He leaned back so she couldn't see his face, but she could see his throat move as he took a long drink from a bottle of water.

"How are you doing today, Miss Osborne?" he asked, wiping the water from his chin with the back of his hand.

"I'm doing great, officer, but I'd like to report an abduction."

"Oh, really. And has this person been missing for twenty-four hours?" He leaned over, smiling down at her, obviously enjoying their banter.

"I'm pretty sure it hasn't been twenty-four hours yet, but I'm sure it will be soon." She managed a cocky smile as if she didn't have a care in the world.

"You're probably right. But then, I'd need the report filed downtown and I don't think you'll have a chance to get down there again."

"Throw down a ladder and I'll race you there," she said.

"Nice try, Sweetheart, but I think I'll keep you."

She sat down, leaning back against the wall with one knee bent as she rested her chin on her knee. Her panic was fading into a sense of resignation. She was going to escape. There wasn't any other option for her, she would find a way. But she wanted to get the story first.

"So you're the brother-in-law?" she said.

"Figured that out, did you?"

"I met your wife, Lily, was it? You probably saw her when you followed me."

Glen laughed harshly. "There wasn't anyone in that tunnel and you know it. And that bitch learned her lesson years ago when I locked her in there."

"Believe what you want, but she told me about Karen." Sloane said.

"What about Karen? About how Alvin was so mad at

~ ☾ ~

her for not loving him he went along with my plan of building the pit you're in right now? It's ingenious, you know."

"I know you think it is." Sloane shifted so she could look up at him. He was getting angry. She probably wasn't being interesting enough for him.

"So, how does this work?" she asked. "You sit there and gloat while I scream for help? But no one can hear me, except maybe the ghosts, so why should I try, right?"

He stared down at her, his eyes contemplative. Sloane sat up a little straighter to see him better. He hadn't shaved in a while and the beginnings of a beard covered his jaw. He scratched at the hair as if it annoyed him.

"Do you know how long it takes for a person to die of thirst?" he asked.

What kind of question was that?

Though it did make her want a tall cool drink just thinking about it.

"I don't know," she told him honestly.

"Starvation takes three weeks. Three long weeks." Glen leaned back in his chair, steepling his fingers before him. He wasn't talking to her anymore. Sloane could tell. He may have even forgotten she was in the room. "And that's too long. Way to long. I can't stand the screams for that long."

There was an eerie gleam of madness in his eyes Sloane could see even from down in the pit.

"Dehydration only takes a week and is much more entertaining."

"Entertaining?"

She should have known better than to ask. She had his full attention again.

"It's very entertaining. You see, first you'll get a headache, similar to when you're hung over. Then your blood pressure will drop, causing you to feel dizzy and possibly faint. I love that part. It's always fun to watch

~ ☾ ~

the victims stumble around. I remember one girl. Freckles, I called her because she had freckles everywhere. She fell down more often than the Three Stooges. I still go back and watch her videos."

If he was waiting for a reaction, Sloane wasn't giving it to him.

"Then comes the delirium. The quiet one with the beautiful big eyes spoke of mirages of water like you'd see in the dessert." His eyes glazed over with memories that seemed to satisfy his sickness. "Alvin liked her. I think she reminded him of Karen. I like to watch this part. The mind makes things up because it wants to believe death isn't near. Quite entertaining. Some see good things. Others just scream. What kind do you think you'll be?"

His eyes snapped back to her. "What horrors will your mind's eye bring you? I can't wait to find out."

She raised one eyebrow at him in mock disdain though inside her soul was screaming in denial.

"After that, you'll probably have periods of unconsciousness before your tongue swells and you finally die. The whole process can take up to a week. I've never had it last longer than that. Frankly, I'd probably get bored if it did because the whole time it's happening, I sit here and I watch the show."

Sloane's mind couldn't quite process the fact that his vindictive plan was now happening to her. All she could think of was the other girls. The spirits trapped here because of the viciousness these men. She'd come to set them free and set them free and now she might become one of them.

Alvin slunk over from the side, standing beside Glen, a cold beer clutched in his hand. He handed the beer to Glen before peering down at her again.

"Where you're sitting right now," there was a touch of pity in Alvin's voice, "that's right where Karen was when she died."

~ ☾ ~

Sloane tried to hide her revulsion but the smile that crept across his face told her she hadn't succeeded.

"I climbed down to cradle her body as she breathed her last breath. I never wanted her to die."

"No, my friend." Glen laid a hand on Alvin's back. "All you asked was for her love and she denied you what you deserved."

"Yes. That exact spot," Alvin continued. "I remember it like yesterday. She couldn't cry—no tears left—so I cried for her."

"You cried for her?" Sloane couldn't keep the disgust out of her voice.

"Of course I did. I'm not a monster. I loved her. If she only been able to see that she loves me too, she wouldn't have had to die at all."

"You're sick. You know that right?"

"So you've told me. Repeatedly. And still you ended up in this trap. Just how I said you would."

He was agitated. Air puffing in and out of him like an angry bear. She was beginning to wonder if the oxygen tank could handle that much use when the sheriff crouched next to him, rubbing his shoulder and murmuring in his ear.

"So I have a question for the both of you," Sloane said.

She was surprised when they turned towards her expectantly.

"Which of the two of you do you think the ghosts are after?"

"There aren't any ghosts." Glen began to turn away but Alvin's eyes locked on her, fear creeping from within their depths.

"Oh there are ghosts," Sloane insisted. "And they are mad. They want revenge. And I think I'm going to side with them when it comes time to battle."

"It didn't say anything online about your mouth," Glen snarled.

~ ☾ ~

"No, it wouldn't." Sloane shook her head in mock dismay. "You can't trust those internet sites, or hadn't you heard that? People can say anything they like about themselves and, unless you meet them, there's no way to find out the truth."

"I think I'm going to be glad when this week is over." Glen's smile was as inhumane as Alvin's. "It'll be the pinnacle of my career when you die in that hole. I'll have lured you here after researching you, discovering you have no one. There won't be anyone to look for you because you are alone. And that's how you like to be."

He'd gotten to her. She hadn't wanted to let him, but he was right. She was alone. The only person who knew where she was or cared was Jonah and he was hundreds of miles away.

"See you know he's right," Alvin sneered. "He's always been the smart one."

"What does it matter to me if he's right? According to you I'm going to die in this hole you put me in. Then you'll burn my body in the incinerator, just like you've done with all the other girls, and I'll be forced to haunt this place forever. At least with you here I'll have someone to harass in the afterlife."

"There's no such thing as ghosts," Glen told her, rising from his seat and helping Alvin away from the pit.

"Keep telling yourself that," Sloane called after them. "But it's still not going to be true."

She heard them shuffle along the floor then a door close somewhere in the room.

"Leave it be, Alvin. She doesn't understand. We've done nothing wrong. Those women were in need of a lesson. I've told you that before and you believed me. This one needs to learn her place more than most. And it's because of you she gets the chance to learn."

"Yes, Glen. I know you're right. I just wish I could shut her up."

~ ☾ ~

"Her tongue will swell soon enough and you'll get to watch the whole thing. Take pride in that."

With that they shut her in blackness, her only companion the blinking red light recording her every sound and movement for two psychos' entertainment. Making a sour face she flipped her middle finger at the blinking red light before sitting down on the floor again.

Moments after their departure, the knocking began.

~ ☾ ~

CHAPTER 8

It began with a thunderous force. All the girls ever trapped in the pit appeared at once banging on the grey cement block walls built around her. They made the ruckus with items they likely died with in the pit. One used her bloodied knuckles, another had broken pieces of glass, one had a spoon, and others used their shoes. One poor girl even kept bashing the concrete with her own head. Sloane backed herself into a corner, trying to stay out of their way.

But they weren't ghosts to Sloane anymore. She felt their corporal bodies when they brushed past her, oblivious to anyone's plight except their own.

A woman Sloane recognized as Karen from the photo in the basement came over and gave Sloane her hand. She had specks of early gray peeking at the edges of her thirty-some temples and deep green eyes that Sloane knew would haunt her until she drew her own last breath. Her dated clothes were ragged and stained. Sloane imagined she was neat and presentable in a sensible and well-tailored suit the day Alvin tossed her in the pit. Now, fragments of a ripped skirt barely covered her knees and her tattered blouse had blood and dirt permanently embedded in it. She removed what was left of her suit jacket and wrapped it around Sloane's shoulders. When the fabric touched her, Sloane enjoyed no extra warmth as the jacket evaporated and reappeared on Karen. Shivers convulsed Sloane's body.

Starvation made her freeze and dehydration burned her up. Her body's energy consumption made her

~ ☾ ~

fluctuate from shivering, to boiling, to achy, to absolute lethargy. Her body was in an over-capacity stress mode. Her irregular heartbeat pounded in her ears.

"I'm sorry I can't do more my dear. I'd say welcome, but some of the girls here won't be very welcoming."

At that, a girl with bloody knuckles and multiple body piercings turned toward Sloane and opened her mouth which held a tongue so swollen that it resembled a mutated slug. Another waif of a thing with sunken in eyes and a long scar down her cheek scratched at the cement until her empty cuticles bled. Dozens of others continued their futile screaming and pounding.

The woman by Sloane's side clapped her hands together sharply like a kindergarten teacher and the girls ceased their commotion and fell silent. "Girls, snap out of it and look around. Be aware. We have another misfortunate soul to help cross over. Can we please make her last days of life in the pit as pleasant as possible?" She made a circle with her index finger and the girls obediently formed a circle around Sloane staring at her with pity and hopelessness in their dead eyes.

Great, they've already written me off for dead and assume I will join their ranks.

Sloane took the woman's hand. Her thigh muscles spasmed as she struggled to her take small steps. "Are you Karen?"

Karen's eyes widened then welled up with tears. "I am, but...how could you...?" she whispered.

Sloane addressed the women surrounding her. "I'm Sloane Osborne. I'm a paranormal investigator and if you help me get out of here, I will make damn sure Alvin and Glen never torture another soul in this God-forsaken pit again. But we need a plan. Who's with me?"

Some of the girls nodded and smiled reaching forward to put a hand on Sloane's shoulder. Others began to bicker among themselves.

"Why help her?" one asked.

~ ☾ ~

"Yeah, who helped us?" said another.

A girl with sunken green eyes and mussed-up dark locks spun in circles looking upward. "I'm still so thirsty. Can she fix that?"

Karen corralled the masses. "Ladies, Sloane is the first one who's been able to see us—talk to us. If we help her, maybe we can end this and be free. Can you help us move on, Sloane?"

"I'll do everything I can, or die trying. As I understand it, if you help me take down your murderer, it will free your spirits and allow you to go to the next plane of existence." Sloane assumed the words she spoke were truth. Jonah said ghosts poked, prodded, and annoyed humans to get their attention. Their real goal was to move on. Jonah had helped many do just that.

Heads began to slowly nod as the girls started to talk amongst themselves and agree.

Sloane limped to the center of the circle, her muscles burning with each painful step. "What's the process here? The sick assholes just sit up there and watch on the camera until we die?"

A dark-skinned girl with a faded denim dress and wavy, boy cut brown hair hung her head. "When I was still alive, but very weak, *he* hauled me up, shoved me in the incinerator and set me on fire while..." Smoke began to rise off of her body as her trauma revisited her. Even slapping at the small pieces of fabric, the flames spread.

The others backed away. The fire spread up her denim outfit and Sloane gagged with the smell of burning flesh and hair. The girl screamed, "Help!" and looked desperately from person to person. Her face charred and hair sizzled. Sloane went to step forward, but Karen held her back. 'Don't," she warned. In less than a minute, she was completely engulfed in flames. In a flash of light, the girl disappeared.

Another girl stepped forward. "Ashley has to relive her last tortured moments every night. Most of us were

~ ☾ ~

unconscious or dead when we were burned and have no memory of the actual pain of our death. We just faded into blackness. But Ashley wasn't so lucky."

Sloane threw her hands up. "This shit will end with me. I swear it. Who's in?" She looked around from face to face. Some were vacant, but most were tough and heavily invested in finally moving their spirits out of this permanent hell hole. "Karen, did you come and help each girl that was in the pit?"

"Like I said before, you're the first one who can see us, talk to us. You're a sensitive. That's why the girls attacked you. After you made first contact by summoning that man ghost—"

"Michael. His name is Michael. He's my fiancé."

Karen gave her a wan smile. "*Was* your fiancé you mean?"

Sloane nodded. "Once Michael showed himself to me, he made me a sensitive. And the gift will be with me forever."

"Gift or curse depending on how you see it and use it. You're in the living world now and can still help us pass on. You said you were willing to help us if we help you. Is that true?" Karen asked.

"I promise to do whatever I can—"

"HEY! Who are you talking to you crazy bitch?" The sheriff poked his head in the hole. "Two days and you're already hearing voices? That was quick!"

"Just chatting up the spirits who are going to send your sick ass to hell, Glen."

"You're a lying sack of shit. There ain't no such thing as ghosts. I never hired you 'cause I thought there was any truth to your bullshit job."

"Are you sure about that, Glen?" She put her hands on her hips. "What are you waiting for? He can't hurt you again. Go say 'hello.'"

Three vanished and shot up as balls of light reappearing in a semi-circle around Glen. One scratched his face

~ ☾ ~

leaving an ugly red welt just short of drawing blood. Another whispered in his ear while the third untied his shoelaces.

Glen jumped straight up in the air, narrowly avoiding falling in the pit with Sloane. "What the..." The coward got his balance back and fled, tripping over his laces as he turned. He scrambled back to his feet as the girls' laughter followed him from the room. His footsteps pounded away.

Single staccato claps came from the control center.

The creaking wheels of Alvin's wheelchair edged toward the top of the pit and the old man leaned his head in. He coughed and spit his bloody sputum into the pit while continuing to clap his hands. "Bravo, my dear. Terrorize him but leave poor innocent me out of this. Be careful you don't make him mad enough to come down there." Alvin held his hand next to his mouth. "He's impotent, you know," he whispered hoarsely.

Had Sloane played right into Alvin hand? Was Glen the pin-pulled-out grenade in Alvin's hand? Did she have any power, even with the ghosts on her side? If Jonah came to investigate, who knew if he'd even find her down here?

With nothing to fight Alvin with but her words, Sloane dug in. "Karen says hi. She's standing right next to me."

Alvin teared up. "Tell her I am sorry. It was an accident. She wasn't supposed to die. Tell her to show herself to me. Why can't I see her?"

Sloane laughed. "And here Glen is convinced the dead don't come back. That burned carcasses don't come back. He's got another thing coming."

"Tell her I shouldn't have gone alone with Glen's plan, but why couldn't she just love me? Like I loved her? I caved to Glen and I have to live with that."

Karen ascended the pit and put a hand on his shoulder.

~ ☾ ~

"She is mine. I should be able to see her! You are not allowed!" Alvin pulled a gun with a huge barrel and fired. Sloane felt something hit her in the shoulder and saw a dart protruding from her skin. Instinctively, she pulled it out. Dart gun? Her shoulder burned then went numb. Sloane sank to the ground willingly so she didn't fall. Her whole body went numb and her vision tunneled. Then everything went black.

When she awoke, she was dazed and her memory foggy. She wondered where she was and why her shoulder hurt. A pounding head, a sick stomach, churning with hunger and worst of all, thirst. The world was on tilt. Her mind whirred, remembering everything, Alvin...Glen...the girls. Her mind whispered horrible thoughts of a quick end to her agony. Dehydration was obviously setting in. She'd fight. Not succumb to its effects.

Voices, gaunt visages, Glen's snarl, and Alvin's gun all haunted her. An overwhelming desire for peace hit her like a sledgehammer to the chest. Now, all she could do was peel her cheek off the cold, slimy cement floor.

Glasses of water surrounded her in a perfect circle. The slivers of light from the basement windows in Glen and Alvin's command center cast an eerie glow on the clear liquid.

Crawling over to one of the glasses, she swirled a finger in the precious liquid. As soon as her finger touched the water, her salivary glands burned and her mind reeled with the almost irresistible desire to drink.

The idea of drinking—anything—threw itself to the forefront of her mind. And these glasses of water were no desert mirage, they were real.

Her moist finger slid across her bottom lip. Just a taste.

Poison? No, that would have been too easy.

It was salt water.

~ ☾ ~

Surrounded with glasses of salt water. Maybe some of the girls hadn't known that drinking it, even if parched, would accelerate the week-long death by dehydration process. She could understand that after a certain point, they might not even care. One by one, she dumped all the glasses so they would offer no temptation and carefully piled them in the corner—never knowing when a girl with an all-state softball pitching arm might get a chance to take out a tooth.

Sloane checked the time on her trusty Mickey Mouse watch. Almost 2:00 a.m. and day two in the pit. Tick tock on the dehydration clock. Five days left? Eight if she was lucky. But with the heat lamps from above, maybe less. Good thing she looked that up in the library after her first encounter with the victims.

Even with her strong survival instinct, motivation to fight left in a hurry without food and water. She gave herself a hard slap. *I'm not dead yet.* The moment she wished for death, that would be it. She needed to keep her wits about her and not give up. Ever. Not an option.

With her head pounding like she had the worst hangover of her life, Sloane crawled to the wall and pulled herself to her feet. The world still felt seriously tilted and plain old wrong. Her vision tunneled from standing up too fast so she sank back to the floor. "Help," she tried to say before she realized that her tongue was twice its regular size and her voice was fast becoming useless. She could no longer yell loud enough for anyone to hear...

When she scratched at her face, white dry flecks of her skin fell off like snow. She pressed the back of her hand to her forehead. She had a fever and her skin burned like she had a bad sunburn. She picked at some loose skin on her forehead. Wanting a long nap, and with her mind foggy and her heart pounding in her head, Sloane only had one thought going through her head, "Michael, save me."

~ ☾ ~

Slowly. Slipping. Away.

Was she beginning to look like the other girls? With her eyes sunken in, skin peeling off, and tongue swollen. Maybe her fate was already sealed. She sank back against the wall and cried without tears. Her limbs tingled from her fingertips and toes and spread up her wrists and ankles to her arms and legs and torso. She needed water. Yesterday.

"Water..." she managed to mumble between sobs.

"I'm sorry sweetie. Did you say something?"

Looking up, Sloane could make out Alvin's profile at the top of the pit. He stirred his ice water and slurped it through a straw. "It's almost beautiful watching you die. It used to bother me, but I'm used to it now. Still, I'm glad you're my last."

She sat motionless, not wanting to alter the scene before her in any way. And yet, at the same time, she needed to sear the images surrounding her into her mind. She needed to summon the strength to live. To exact revenge for these girls. She closed her eyes and imagined herself on a beach with Michael...

The sun-speckled waves rolled in and out with a dull roar. Crescendo and decrescendo. Gulls squawked in the distance and palm trees swayed with the afternoon breeze.

Lifting her hand which was interlocked with Michael's, she closed her eyes and inhaled the smell of sea salt mixed with his cologne. His skin was warm from the sun. A sudden whip of wind blew her long, hair over her face and obscured her vision.

After releasing her hand, Michael brushed away the offending strands. Shade settled over her face. Her hair became a nemesis she would defeat even if she had to cut it all off right now. How dare it block her view of him?

Michael was above her.

~ ☾ ~

"Open your eyes, silly."

She wanted to see his face again almost as much as she wanted it erased from her mind forever. When his caramel eyes stared at her, she was consumed by him. He could look at her and make her feel as though nothing else existed in the universe except their love.

She opened her eyes.

His strong cheeks, dirty blond hair, and the bane of her existence...his perpetual sexiness. Michael's eyes bored into her soul and she allowed it. Her throat tightened and a weight pushed on her chest like a heavy boulder ready to smother her. "How do you like this beach?" His voice and heat sent a ripple of pleasure through her.

Michael intertwined their hands again and pulled her to a sitting position.

Palm trees fanned out behind them. The beach paradise stretched for miles in both directions. "It's perfect. How long do we have?"

"I'm here for as all long as you need until I can give you enough strength to get through this. Why? You have somewhere better to be?" His eyes twinkled and he raised an eyebrow.

She bit her lip and shook her head. No, this hallucination was the perfect place to be.

Then they were in the turquoise water.

She held her breath and let her body sink into the crystal clear water. They found each other's hands. Michael squeezed hers.

But the scene faded. Fast. The clouds darkened, then sky opened. Michael was fading away.

"There's no point to this Sloane. I need you to wake up and fight. Fight for this future for every other woman Glen will torture and kill if you don't beat him. Then let me go, Sloane. Go live your life. That's what I want for you my love."

She squeezed his hands but her vision tunneled

~ ☾ ~

around her going black from the outside in. Then his hands were gone and she was alone, fists clenched, staring up at Glen.

His aura of grotesqueness was nearly palatable. He oozed hatred for her in his dilated black pupils. His dirt-stained hands gripped his pristine glass of water as he balanced on the two back legs of his wooden chair rocking precariously close to the edge of her dungeon. He set down his water and picked up a guitar and began to play some kind of Baroque or Renaissance song.

The scene was comical to Sloane. Her would-be killer serenading her with his classical guitar. She laughed out loud.

"I'm pretty fucking awesome, aren't I?" Glen's voice echoed through a small intercom in the wall. "Studied with a strict asshole who'd slap me with a ruler when my fingering wasn't just so. This is my interpretation of 'Come Away' by John Dowland. He was a Renaissance composer whose use of melody was severely overlooked by the average guitarist." Glen finished his piece and set down the instrument. "I picked you myself you know."

Sloane kept quiet. He was chatty and he and bound to give away something he shouldn't. Maybe something she could use.

"I did my research. After your fiancé died, you did nothing. You died anyway. I thought I'd give you the kick in the ass you needed. Paranormal real estate agent?" Glen spat and chuckled. "That's a fucking idea that works. Not. You are useless, hopeless, and chasing after some dead guy you think is going to poof into a haunted house and say 'hi'?"

Sloane suppressed the urge to say, "Yuppers, Glen. That was exactly what happened." She kept her eyes locked on his.

Glen picked up the guitar again. "Now that Fed was a surprise. But it was no problem getting rid of him with a quick call with my anonymous tip." He began another

~ ☾ ~

Renaissance piece leaving Sloane feeling like she should don a heavy wool dress, underskirt, and a linen headdress.

Poor Jonah was called away for nothing. By Glen. She was alone with an army of skittish but pissed off ghosts.

"But he ran away to answer the call of duty. With your parents dead, you being an only child with no damn friends to speak of and a career of solitude looking for ghosts, I loved the idea of having you be my first hand selected victim."

He had researched every detail of her life. *Psycho.* Her heart began to beat harder. Scary how easy it was for him to find out every detail of her life, who she was, her family. He didn't believe in ghosts... yet.

Glen continued with his music while Sloane finalized the plan of her escape before the last of her brain cells failed her.

~ ☾ ~

CHAPTER 9

Shifting restlessly on the cold, hard floor Sloane didn't know if hours or days had passed. Time began to blur. From the filthy dry scum coating her mouth, she would guess more than a day. In and out of dreams. Hallucinating mostly, and it angered her that she had let herself get this way. She was a fighter, not someone who sat back and succumbed to the inevitable.

Each time she was able to surface, to drag what was left of her mind back to coherency, she had only one thought; she had to escape.

Impossible though it seemed, that was the only option she would allow herself to consider. She couldn't let Glen or Alvin win. They'd won too many times already and she wasn't going to let herself become a tally on their chart.

She needed a plan.

Through dry eyes that could no longer form tears, she blinked up at the light above her taking stock of her assets. She had a few broken glasses, her clothes, and her brain. Not much to work with. She could try to make a rope from her clothes, but the perverts would probably enjoy the show.

It would have to be the ladder.

But how would she get the ladder down into the hole? That was the big question.

From where she sat, leaning against the smooth edge of the hole, she could barely see the emergency ladder case they had waiting at the top of her prison. There was no way she could reach it. She'd have to bait one of them

~ ☾ ~

into coming into the hole with her. That was the only way.

She cleared her throat roughly, testing before she spoke.

"Hey, Asshole." Her voice came out as a hoarse whisper. "Can you come over here a minute?"

There was a scuffling of hasty movement. He must not have known she was awake. Someone wasn't paying attention to his cameras.

The sheriff sauntered over to the hole, his belly hugged by the too tight button down uniform shirt, his badge a mockery on his chest.

"Are you talking to me?" he asked. "Because I can't hear you. If you want to talk to me, speak into the intercom."

Sloane pulled herself to her feet, using the wall for support and spoke into the small mic embedded in the wall. "Why don't you come down here for a minute?"

"I don't think so." He turned to walk away.

"Yeah, I figured you were too much of a pansy to fight me straight up. You have to drain your opponents first."

His fist clenched at his side. She knew his kind. Evil and full of themselves. Usually easy to anger and not much going on in the head. Her only hope was to get him so mad he had to prove himself and come down in the hole with her.

With slow, measured movements, she pulled one of the broken glasses into her hand, ready to use if he was dumb enough to fall for her plan.

"I don't want to fight you, Sloane." Glen's voice was too calm. She bit her lip, tasting blood. It wasn't working. She'd have to try harder.

"No, you just want to watch me," she said. "Is that how you get off? Can't get any so you have to play by yourself?"

She heard the water bottle crunch as he fisted his hands again.

~ ☾ ~

"I don't need to play by myself. Before we're done, you'll be begging me to take you. And for what? Just a sip of this." He poured the rest of his water on the ground. A few drops splashed down into the hole and Sloane watched them soak into the ground with passive disgust. Such a waste.

"Here you go, Sloane. Drink up." He tossed the now empty bottle down, a few drops of the precious water hitting her in the cheek.

"Haha. Very funny." Cursing herself for her need, she reached for the bottle. Tipping it back and catching the last bit on her swollen tongue. When she looked up, he was still watching her from the edge of the hole.

"It's going to be fun to watch you die." His voice was quiet, almost as if he was talking to himself. "One of the best."

Sloane hugged her arms around her middle, the edges of her vision beginning to fade as panic took over. She forced herself to breathe. In, out. In, out. Nice steady breaths.

Glen was not the answer then. She'd have to wait. Bide her time, or what little she had until she was alone with Alvin. Though she never thought to say it, he was the weak link and he was her only chance of survival.

She laughed at the irony. Alvin the fucking psycho was her only chance of survival.

She didn't even try to fight it when exhaustion claimed her again. Her dreams, or hallucinations, were far better than a conversation with Glen.

Throwing her keys on the small table by the door, Sloane sighed as she switched on the light. She was home first. Not always the case but much appreciated tonight. She wanted a nice hot shower and a few minutes to find herself before Michael got home. It had been a long, tiring week, between her full time job and school, she needed a break.

The warm water running over her skin was

~ ☾ ~

intoxicating. It slid down her skin like a liquid caress and she ran her hands down her body, savoring the feel of the water as it soaked into her thirsty soul.

Why was she so thirsty?

The answer was there but she couldn't hold on to it.

"Where are you?" a voice whispered in her head. A voice she knew but she didn't have the strength to answer.

Sloane screamed, throwing her hands out to cover herself as the shower curtain was jerked back and male hands reached for her.

His laughter calmed her. Michael. It was only Michael.

"Come here," he called playfully. "I need a welcome home kiss."

"But you're getting all wet."

"I'll dry."

And his lips were on hers. She closed her eyes, savoring the taste that was so uniquely him. Like vanilla and honey, aphrodisiacs to her. One taste and she was lost to him forever.

He let her go before she was ready, pulling off his shirt and dropping it, wet, onto the linoleum floor.

"Hurry and get out. Get dressed in something nice. We need to celebrate."

Sloane reluctantly turned off the tap water, frowning at the sudden ache the action caused in her chest.

Why was the water so important?

"Where are you?" she heard the voice again, but was too focused on Michael to respond.

He was so gorgeous. With a shock of dirty blonde hair that always fell into his bright blue eyes and a facial structure and body that would make a Greek God stare and groan, he was utter perfection and he was hers. All hers. Or he would be as soon as they were married next month.

"What's so important you can't let me shower in peace?"

~ ☾ ~

"Besides wanting to see your raging hot body? Do I need any other reason?"

She smiled at him as she wrapped a towel around her hair, waiting for the real answer.

"All right," he said. "We had a break through today and it's the most amazing thing."

Sloane perked up in real interest. Michael worked for a pharmaceutical company and was on a team of researchers developing a new cancer drug. Anything that had him this excited must have amazing effects.

"It's not ready for trials on humans yet, but we're almost there and this is it. I feel it. This is the drug that's going to take down brain cancer and keep people alive."

"That's amazing, Michael. I'm so proud of you."

"Proud enough to splurge on dinner at Garbazios?" He knew she could never say no to their favorite restaurant.

"I'll just get dressed." She sidled past him as he turned on the water again.

Telling herself it was a special occasion, Sloane poured herself a glass of wine to sip on while she dressed. It was only a stale white but the liquid on her throat was like ambrosia. She felt her body come to life just from that one bit of fluid on her tongue.

She paused, putting a hand to her head. Something wasn't right here. What was going on?

"Where are you?" She heard the voice again and this time knew it was Jonah. But why was he in her head? "How do I find you? Sloane, you need to help me here."

"The recliner." She couldn't remember why, but she knew it was important. "In the basement."

She staggered and almost fell, spilling some of the precious wine on the carpet.

"Dammit." She pulled the towel off her head and used it to dab at the liquid of the floor.

Sloane dressed carefully, though she did try to hurry. Knowing what a special celebration entailed, she took

~ ☾ ~

extra care of her body, smearing on the peach lotion Michael loved and taking her time with her makeup. Her hair would never dry in time so she pulled in back in a tight chignon, leaving a few wispy strands to softly frame her face.

Sliding into a short black dress and knock-em-dead high heels, she paused to glance at herself in the mirror.

She looked pretty good, if she did say so herself.

And suddenly her heart hurt just looking at herself. An ache deep inside there was no hiding from. She wanted to cry but couldn't remember why. She just had the feeling she hadn't looked this good or wanted to in a long time. But that couldn't be right. She always wanted to look sexy for Michael.

The only thing that would make that change was if she lost him.

Her head swam and she smelled the dirt and dank of a basement. Where was she? She couldn't remember anymore. She heard Jonah's voice again and knew something was horribly wrong. This wasn't real. Michael couldn't be here.

He was dead.

She not only seen his body lain out in the casket, but had made contact with his ghost. This wasn't real, but she wanted it to be so bad.

Movement in the mirror captured her attention and distracted her from the ache tearing through her chest. Michael strode in the room, a dark green towel resting lazily on his hips. She felt her nipples harden to tight peaks and wetness seep between her legs just looking at him. Those rock hard abs and sculpted chest. How did a science geek get to look like that?

Her mouth watered for a taste.

"Dammit, Sloane, where are you?" Jonah's voice was loud in her mind this time. "I need to find you before it's too late."

But she couldn't respond. All of her attention was

~ ☾ ~

riveted on Michael as droplets of water slowly made their way down his chest to disappear into the towel.

"My God, you're beautiful," he said.

She hadn't noticed that he was staring at her with the same soul-searing love in his eyes she knew was in hers.

"I can't believe you're actually mine." Michael wrapped his arms around her waist, gazing at her in the mirror.

She smiled, shifting provocatively from one stiletto to the other.

"Well, you'd better get used to it because everything is planned. All we need is that one silly marriage license and I'll be as good as yours."

"Tomorrow." He strode towards her, his hand going behind her neck to tip her head back. "We'll go get it tomorrow."

For a moment while his lips slowly descended towards hers, Sloane couldn't breathe. Clear as day she could see him before her, his eyes glassy in death. She wanted to cry, but couldn't summon the tears. Then his lips were on hers and she forgot about everything else.

This was Michael touching her, kissing her, bringing her as close to heaven as she could ever imagine being.

His mouth was like a brand on her, and he eased his tongue along the seam of her lips until she opened for him, his tongue sliding inside to dance with her own. His hand slid up her thigh and under her dress, coming to rest on the curve of her buttocks. He groaned into her mouth, pulling away to rest his forehead against hers.

"Sweetheart, tell me you have something on under that dress," he whispered, his eyes closed.

"You said it was a special occasion." She couldn't stop touching him, nibbling along his jaw while she smiled at his reaction. "Besides, where would I put anything under this?"

She was suddenly in his arms, being swept up towards their bed.

~ ☾ ~

"I think we'll order in tonight." His voice was rough as he placed her carefully in the center of the bed.

"And I was so looking forward to going out," she teased.

He shed the towel before joining her, covering her with his larger frame like a warm blanket. She wrapped herself around him, reveling in the length and hardness she found pressed against her most intimate part. There was something almost decadent about him naked while she was almost fully clothed.

His hands slid up her sides, caressing her through the thin black material, finding her breasts. Her nipples were so hard and sensitive she thought she would orgasm with just his touch, but when his mouth closed around one round peak through the fabric of her dress, she arched off the bed, forcing herself closer to the heat and touch.

"God, Sweetheart. You're so ready for me. Are you wet down here too?"

His hand trailed slowly down her stomach to cup her between the thighs.

"You don't know how hot it is when a woman is already wet for her man."

He slid one finger into her and she moaned, feeling the heat pooling between her legs.

"Maybe we'll skip dinner altogether and I'll just have you, again and again, all night long."

Sloane could do nothing but agree as he slid down, pushing her dress up past her waist to angle himself between her thighs. He didn't wait for an invitation, but his tongue plunged inside of her, sinking deep, before retracting to play at her most sensitive area. Her fingers tunneled into his hair, holding her to him as her body spiraled out of control. She clung to him as he feasted, feeling the tension building until she was at her breaking point.

Then he was there. The soft thickness pushing into

~ ☾ ~

her, stretching her, and filling her. He was as out of control as she felt, pumping into her hard and fast while she writhed beneath him, begging for more. It had always been like this between the two of them. Carnal and full of emotion, but this time there was desperation to their lovemaking she didn't remember feeling before. She had to have him, all of him, body and soul, and it had to be now. Or never again.

She screamed as an orgasm tore through her, her channel tightening around him, milking him as he drove on in his quest for fulfillment. Her lips found his shoulder and she nibbled along his collar bone, leaving small bites she soothed with a swirl of her tongue. The tension was building again and she could feel herself losing control.

As a second orgasm tore through her, shattering her control, she felt him stiffen as he climaxed inside her. She rode the waves of his love as her body began to settle and he shifted her to one side to keep from crushing her smaller frame beneath his weight. She sighed, snuggling into him, her head resting on his shoulder.

Amazing.

She was glad they weren't going out anymore. She couldn't imagine sitting in a restaurant with him right now, wishing he could do all those wonderful things to her again but knowing she had to wait for the bill. She wanted him again. And again. Over and over all night long, just like he'd said. She wanted to eat take-out naked in bed and just look at him, memorizing his smile, the sound of his voice, the fall of his hair.

"I love you, Sloane. You know that, right?" he whispered in her ear, his hand straying to rest possessively over her breast.

"Of course I know"

"No matter what happens in the future, you have to know what I'll love you forever."

~ ☾ ~

She lifted her head to look at him, suddenly worried.

"Why does it sound like you're saying good-bye to me?"

"I could never say good-bye to you." He pulled her head down to his as his mouth leisurely explored hers. "That's part of the problem."

"What problem?"

His smile was sad as he touched her face and she could already feel him fading.

"Michael, what are you talking about?"

"You could stay with me, Sloane. If you want. We could make it work."

Stay with him? Of course, she was going to stay with him? What was he talking about? Tomorrow they would go get the marriage license and they would get married and live happily ever after.

That's how these things worked.

"Sloane," Jonah's voice was like a knife in her head, cutting through the smog and reaching to her soul. For a moment she could see him in Alvin's basement. "What do you mean the chair? It's just a damn chair." He kicked the offending piece of furniture.

"Pull the lever, idiot." She shot back at him.

As he reached down to do that, his image faded and she was back in bed, the sheets pulled over her chest.

She sat up, gazing down at Michael where he lay beside her.

"This isn't real, is it?"

"No," Michael admitted. "It's a memory, but a good memory. I'm glad you remember me this way."

"Am I dying?" she asked.

"You could," Michael said. "You could die right now. I could help you. We could be together forever and all the pain would be gone."

Sloane looked around the room, but even as she did the walls of her old apartment began to fade and she saw the cool gray walls of her prison surrounding her. She

~ ☾ ~

huddled on the floor, curled into herself. Squeezing her eyes shut, she willed herself back to the dream and Michael was there.

"I'm not going anywhere, Sloane." He reached out, running a finger down her cheek and tucking her hair behind her ear. "Not until you've decided."

"The other girls?" she asked. "What will happen to them?"

"Nothing. They will remain exactly as they are."

So they would be stuck and Glen would be free to kill again.

"Don't you give up on me, Sloane." She heard Jonah in her head again. "Don't go with him. I need you here. You know I do."

He was angry and she knew why. It was so tempting to just give in. To let Michael take her pain away and take care of her again. But she couldn't do it.

"I love you, Michael."

Michael's eyes grew sad as he looked into her eyes.

"You're not going to stay with me, are you?" Michael asked.

"I can't." She wished things were different but they weren't and she couldn't allow all of those girls to continue to suffer. And Jonah was right. He needed her.

He kissed her forehead, pulling her head down onto his shoulder again. His sigh was so heartbreaking Sloane wanted to cry, but for some reason she couldn't summon the tears. She felt the burning behind her eyes and the painful lump in her throat but she couldn't release the emotion.

"I always knew you'd choose him," he whispered.

She heard a cry of agony from somewhere in the distance and shifted on the bed. Only the soft mattress and warm body next to her was gone. She was cold and uncomfortable on the floor.

"Sloane," she heard Jonah's voice in her head again, this time almost like a caress. As if he sensed the

~ ☾ ~

anguish and turmoil in her. "You have to tell me where you are. I need to find you."

"I'm still here," she said. "Through the tunnel."

She opened her eyes, shuttering at the sight around her. The broken glasses still stacked to one side of her smooth, round cage. The soft electric light sifting down from above where someone watched her. She felt eyes on her now. And not Michael or Jonah's.

She sat up slowly, fighting the waves of dizziness threatening to pull her back under again.

"You're amusing when you sleep." Glen's voice was strained, as if it was difficult to speak.

Glancing up at him, she saw the problem. He was now sitting in a metal folding chair just at the edge of the pit, his hand working up and down inside his pants.

"Can you moan for me again, girl? I like it when you moan."

Sloane's only response was to pick up half of a broken glass and lob it up at him. She hadn't been the starting pitcher on her college softball team for nothing. The glass made a loud thunking noise when it struck Glen square in the forehead, leaving a small bloody mark behind.

Sloane wished it had done more damage.

Glen swore, his hand coming out of his pants to cover the wound.

"Stupid bitch. I should keep you asleep more often. It's the only time you do anything worth watching."

Sloane didn't try to talk. She'd spend the rest of her miserable existence both as a human or a ghost trying to thwart his every move. It was all she had left to look forward to.

"At least I have it on video," he smirked down at her. "So I can watch you writhing and moaning any time I want. Dreaming of your fiancé, maybe? You're dead fiancé? Or was it your pretty boy from the government?"

~ ☾ ~

He paused, as if he actually thought she rise to his bait.

"It doesn't matter. Neither one can save you now."

The look in his eyes was cold. Like the murderer he was.

"Take your time dying down there, girl."

~ ☾ ~

CHAPTER 10

Now Sloane was pissed. Glen was talking about getting off to a video of her dying. And there was nothing she could do to stop him. No way was she going to die at the hands of this loser and sulk with these other lost souls for eternity. Time to summon the last functioning brain cells she had left...

"So Glen," she rasped into the intercom. "How long did it take that girl last year to die?"

Glen grimaced. Shadows covered his face. He leaned out, resting his hand on the thick cord that held the lantern lighting her dungeon. It creaked, not used to the movement as it swung to and fro. "Ten days. She fell into a coma or something. She didn't move much after day seven." He paused and gave Sloane an evil grin that made her skin crawl. "But I found a way to wake her up. Why? Wondering how much longer you got?"

Sloane shifted so her face was under the hanging lamp. She squinted up at him past the glaring light reflecting off the smooth walls of her cement prison. "Maybe." Each dry word burned her throat but she knew she had to keep him talking. "Then what will happen to me? Alvin sends you down to retrieve the dead body and burn it. Must suck being his minion, hey?" Sloane's mind spun. She was desperate to goad Glen into doing something—anything.

"I'm nobody's lackey you dumb bitch. And that slut last year sure as hell wasn't dead. Screamed her ass off while I watched her burn. Alvin's on his death bed. Besides this always has been, and always will be...my gig."

~ ☾ ~

"But for what? What's your spin on this? I don't get it." Sloane knew about Lily, but it still felt like there was a piece missing.

Glen's face changed. She'd struck a chord.

He mumbled something incoherent.

"What?" Sloane held her hand up to her ear.

In a barely audible whisper, Glen said, "I'm not pathetic like Alvin who pined for a woman who never wanted him. Women annoy me. They're only good for one thing. I give the good ones sips of water in the end to keep them going if they please me. Are you going to try to please me?" He flashed an evil grin.

An image flashed in Sloane's mind. The girl down here that was set on fire...while still alive. What was her name? She was the newest addition to the pit. Could she be Glen's Karen?

Sloane spun around to find the girl who'd kept going up in flames. "Ashley!" Sloane whispered. Fitting name for the poor girl.

A tug on her sleeve. Sloane jumped and found Ashley behind her.

"Tell me your story. It might help."

She nodded. *"I not proud of this, but I was having an affair. The wife broke in and trashed my place when she found out. I'd filed a police report about it and Glen came to investigate. While he was interviewing me, he asked me out and I reported him."* Her voice was barely above a whisper in the wind. *"Because of me, he almost got fired. But they took his word over mine. His co-workers all got a good laugh over it."*

The girl hung her head as the wisps of smoke again began to appear on her hands. This time she didn't scream. She tipped her head back and let the flames engulf her, like an ill-accused witch tied to the stake bravely suffering through her appointed date with death.

"You're the judge and jury now? Punishing Ashley for

~ ☾ ~

her sins? Or for turning you down and making fun of you?"

He glared at her. "Who told you that? I don't know what you're talking about."

She had him. Sloane needed Glen in that pit with her by any means necessary and she was prepared to do... or say...

Oh, who the hell was she fooling?

"Glen." Sloane used a tone she reserved for Michael. But Michael would forgive her the indiscretion if it saved her life. But before she could utter another word, a wave of dizziness came over her. Her head spun. Bouts like this came frequently now, anytime she expended too much energy. She sank to the cold floor. Maybe death would be preferable. At least she'd be reunited with Michael.

If Glen came down in the pit and her plan backfired, she be raped and die at the hands of a psychopath. But if she didn't try, others would die after her.

I have to try. She breathed deeply to clear her foggy head and muster some mental reserve energy.

"Glen. I don't think you're so bad. Since my fiancé died, I've been so... lonely." She almost choked on her words. Holding up one hand she watched it shake before squeezing it into a fist to hide it from Glen. She didn't have much time. "I wouldn't mind if you came down here."

He shifted on his feet but his brow slowly unfurrowed. His expression softened into something almost human.

"Get his sorry ass down here!" Ashley looked like she was out for blood.

Sloane spun her head around to see Ashley, on fire but moving toward her. *"Get him down here so I can..."* She balled her fist and threw a ball of fire at the floor next to Sloane. Heat radiated from the spot warming Sloane's hands and face. The girl's anger gave her fuel and her flame ball had been real.

~ ☾ ~

Fire traveled up Ashley's arm and spread throughout her torso. Screaming once again in her perpetual torment, Ashley disappeared.

"What are you looking at?" Glen asked.

Sloane reengaged with Glen. "Come down here."

He shook his head. "You just want to save yourself. You're a lying bitch. No one loves you and no one will care when you are dead. Shut up. I'm out of here."

"Wait!"

Sloane had nothing.

"Stop talking to the killer." One of the girls warned.

"Why are you being so nice to him?" She was confused.

The ghosts surrounded her. Now they were all angry at her.

"Help me out here, girls. I'm bluffing," she whispered to the ghosts. They melted into the background. "You probably don't know what to do with a woman anyway. You couldn't handle Lily or even Ashley, and you wouldn't be able to handle me! You probably don't even have functioning machinery in those pants, do you? Ashley told me everything."

Glen whipped around, knelt down, and grabbed the side of the pit with his hands and leaned in. "How do you know about Ashley? In the end, I showed her the only thing a woman's good for—kindling. You want the same? You want to be burned alive too?"

"So you burn women who reject you? I'm *asking* you to come down here. You probably couldn't satisfy me if you tried. Are you a limp noodle, Glen?"

"Shut up."

Sloane goaded him like a five year old. "Limp noodle Glen. That's what I'll call you."

He disappeared and a ladder descended into the pit. Not the emergency ladder they kept by the ledge, but an actual aluminum extension ladder someone would use to get on their roof. Sloane's heart began to thump.

~ ☾ ~

That's how she'd escape.

Sloane grabbed one of the sharp pieces of glass she kept handy for such an occasion. Her plan involved stabbing Glen in the jugular and getting the hell out of Dodge.

He descended the ladder mumbling, "First I'm going to bash your brain in. Then I'll burn you alive. Dumb whore-slut-bitch."

Sloane pressed her back up against the far wall which felt cold as death. "Ladies, might need some assistance here."

Karen appeared right next to her. *"We're here Sloane."*

Emboldened by the ghostly army appearing around her, Sloane dropped her eyes from Glen. "I'm sorry. I... I didn't mean it. Please Glen, don't hurt me."

He jumped down, skipping the last few rungs and was in front of her. His breath on her face reeked with an acrid stench of rotted cigarettes and old whiskey.

Now that she was this close to him, she felt the evil radiate from him. Had she underestimated his resolve? Unlike Alvin, coming to the end of a life of horror, Glen was damn agile for his fifties. He made his victims thirst for water like he thirsted to cause pain.

He chewed on his lip. "Oh now you're sorry? First you flirt, then you call me a limp noodle. Oh yeah, I forgot. You're a woman. You LIE!" He pressed his hands on the wall on either side of Sloane, pinning her between him.

"No. I wasn't lying," Sloane purred before slamming her fist into his throat and kneeing him in the groin. Glen slumped forward and Sloane made a dash for the ladder. At the same time, her ghostly army surrounded Glen. She caught a glimpse of Ashley's burning hand reaching out to grab him.

He shouted in pain. She risked a glance back and saw a smoldering black handprint on the fabric of his shirt.

Three rungs until the top.

~ ☾ ~

Two.

Last one.

Her hand got pummeled with something hard—a hammer? She looked up into Alvin's twisted face. He pushed the ladder backward and it slammed into the other side of the pit before Sloane lost her grip and tumbled to the ground in a heap. Her ankle screamed in pain and the breath was knocked out of her. The ghosts surrounded Glen's still screaming form where he writhed on the ground.

The last thing she saw before she slid into unconsciousness was Alvin pulling up the ladder, blocking her escape and sealing her fate.

When she woke up, both the ladder and Glen were long gone and the ghosts were pacing and arguing amongst themselves.

"The ladder is the only way out."

"Alvin and Glen need to be punished."

"She can punish them."

Groggy from the fall, Sloane sat up and reached for her twisted ankle. It throbbed and pounded with pain. The dehydration had taken hold and her mind swirled in a haze. She given a valiant effort, hadn't she? Maybe if she let her mind slip away, her body would follow. She muttered the only word that mattered. "Water."

The girls crowded her. When they touched her, she couldn't really feel it, but she felt something, like the satin touch of a clean sheet shaken above you and the whisper soft touch it leaves when it lands on your body. Karen stepped forward and placed a hand on her brow.

"There, there. Rest, or you won't have enough strength. Girls, give her some room." She told the others before turning her attention back to Sloane. *"You have some good reason to live, don't you dear?"*

Sloane nodded. "Jonah."

Sloane let herself slip away again into a half dream of

~ ☾ ~

when Michael was still her boyfriend and Jonah hadn't
yet left for D.C. ...

She and Jonah were paired up again this weekend on
the paranormal investigative team assignment. The
abandoned house on Concord Street had been called in
as a location with possible paranormal activity. They got
comfortable on the dusty oak floor in the hallway of the
house. Reports of suspicious noises had been heard in
the past by trespassing kids who'd posted it on the web.
The real estate agent trying to sell the place wanted the
myth squelched so she could dump the property. Sloane
had recently finished her own real estate license and had
started working at a local agency.

Jonah covered her legs with a blanket. Their breaths
changed to puffs of smoke in the cold Illinois air.
Somehow being next to him made her feel safe. He
switched on the equipment and scanned the hallway in
his ever watchful mode.

"So when are you getting a ring on that finger?" he
asked.

"Michael says as soon as I stop wasting my time
hunting the dead, he'll help me start to live. He wants
me to promise I'll stop ghost hunting after we're
engaged so we can spend more time together."

Jonah turned to her with a look in his eyes like his
dog had died. "But you love doing this. It's our monthly
meeting to catch up with each other. This group
wouldn't be any fun without out."

She sighed. He was right. This group was one of the
best parts of her life, she loved it and it gave her a
chance to chill with Jonah and see how he was doing.
She considered him her best friend too and it was nice to
have it be just the two of them sometimes. This was the
only time they every hung out without Michael. She
sometimes wondered if Michael was jealous. But she
was about to be engaged and would have to plan a

~ ☾ ~

wedding and that meant changing for the other person, didn't it?

"This is actually my last time, Jonah. I'll miss it, too. But I have to do what Michael wants and he thinks this is silly. You know, I've never really seen anything to prove the existence of ghosts. I just happen to believe you."

After Jonah's first contact, he could sense and see spirits—good and bad ones. Sloane believed him like she believed in gravity and God. Jonah had no reason to lie to her and he was the most trustworthy person she knew, one of those guys who thought about everyone before himself.

Jonah turned off the recording devices and stole some of her blanket to cuddle around both of them, making her insides tingle when their jeans brushed against each other. She pulled away, knowing she was about to marry his best friend and shouldn't feel anything more than friendship with Jonah. "I won't second guess you. If you are doing it to make Michael happy, I totally support you. But can I ask you something?"

"Anything." The blanket smelled of pine needles. Jonah kept that blanket in the back of his pickup truck which sat out under the evergreens in his yard.

"You and I have a weird connection, right?"

She nodded. They did even though they'd never talked about it.

"Do me a favor. Think about me right now. Funny me. Drunk me. Whatever me. But close your eyes and concentrate. I'm going to do the same."

"But why—"

"Just trust me, Sloane."

"That's funny coming from the guy who trusts very few people."

"Please." His eyes said something to quiet her and she obeyed.

~ ☾ ~

A picture came to her mind of her jumping out to surprise Jonah. They were staking out a location and she snuck around the house and came up from behind and tickled his right side. He'd jumped in the air and almost hit her when he spun around.

Sloane had never let him live it down that she'd scared him.

That's when she felt it.

Hands squeezing her shoulders.

She leaned toward Jonah. It couldn't be him though because he was still sitting right next to her. "Uh, Jonah..."

"Yes, Sloane..."

"Something's touching me."

"Where?"

She lowered her voice. "Squeezing my shoulders."

Whatever it was that was squeezing her shoulders, it wasn't Jonah. Sloane's eyes snapped open and she jumped up. "I felt something! A ghost! It put its hands on my shoulders and squeezed! That was so cool! Did you feel anything? Do we have the recording equipment on?"

Jonah looked at the floor. "It was me."

"It couldn't have been. You didn't move."

"I was concentrating on that time we were dart partners when your friend Jody was paired up with Michael. Remember how before each shot, I'd squeeze your shoulders for luck?"

"Yeah, but wait... you... whoa." What Jonah was capable of doing, how he could connect with her, finally clicked.

Jonah turned to face her and his eyes bore into her. It was a look she had never seen from him before. Like looking at her was the only thing he could possibly do. His eyes roamed from her hair, to her cheeks, to her lips.

Electricity passed through her. "Did you feel anything from me?" she asked.

~ ☾ ~

"Yeah, on my right side, like you were grabbing at me, or tickling me. You weren't thinking about that time you thought you scared me, were you?"

Sloane nodded. Was this kind of connection possible between two people? "Whoa. You're serious about this?"

He looked up at her. "Dead serious. Sloane, I—" His eyes settled again on her lips and for one small moment, seared in her memory, she knew it was Jonah that made her heart skip. Jonah that should have bought her that first drink in the bar. But she had pushed the thought to the back of her mind and left it there ever since.

She never knew what he was about to say. Three other members of their crew traipsed up the stairs all excited about capturing orbs photos in the basement...

Sloane felt the hard concrete on her cheek and blinked. Her eyes stung without tears to lubricate them. She heard his voice in her head again.

"Sloane! Where are you?" Jonah voice was loud and clear.

With every ounce of energy she could muster, she concentrated on her surroundings hoping Jonah would be able to see it too. The connection was the key. If anyone could find her, it was him.

Then she felt it.

Someone's hands on her shoulders.

~ ☾ ~

CHAPTER 11

Jonah was close. She knew it. He had to be or she wouldn't be able to feel him. Trying to sit up, she grimaced in agony. Her entire body hurt from her twisted ankle to the throbbing headache pounding inside her brain. Propping herself against the edge of her prison, she closed her eyes again, wishing the next time she opened them, the pounding behind her eyes would be gone and she would be in a little bar on a beach with a drink in her hand.

No such luck.

"I can see your really awake now," she heard Glen call down to her. "And as you can see I'm not down in your pit. You lose. I win. Just the way it's supposed to be."

"Shut up, Glen." Ger voice was hoarse and raspy, every word grating through her dry throat, past bloody lips. "I'm trying to figure out how to die with some dignity down here, so leave me alone."

He had the nerve to laugh at her as he walked away.

She laughed as well.

She was dying. What she thought she wanted since Michael left her. She never acted on it, because deep down she knew there was more to life than being with him. She loved him, but he didn't hold the other half of her soul. Joining Michael now was the easy thing to do.

But now that she teetered on the brink of the abyss, she didn't want to die. There was still something... or someone... holding her to this world.

Literally.

~ ☾ ~

With a hand on her shoulder.

"Jonah," she whispered.

Was he out there? Looking for her? Oblivious to the fact two murderers held her captive? If they dumped her in a hole to watch her die, killing Jonah would be nothing to them.

He could not die. She wouldn't allow it.

"It's about time you realized that."

Her eyes snapped open in shock. That old, familiar voice.

"Michael," she sighed.

In that moment, memories flooded her mind. The way he made her feel, like the sun shone only for her. How his smile blanketed her in warmth on a cold winter day. God dammit, how much she missed him.

Her heart carried a never-ending ache. A clear thought hit her. It was not yet her time to join him. And the pain and ache she carried missing him would never abate. A part of her would always belong to him.

Damn. Even transparent, he still looked good.

A sad smile crossed his face. He cupped her cheek in his hand. She could almost feel it.

Almost.

But not quite.

"Sloane," he said softly. "You look like hell."

She sniffed.

"Of course I do. I'm trapped in a hole and literally dying of thirst. Get off my case."

"Okay, okay." His grin was still the lopsided smile she remembered. "Always the sarcasm."

"Are you here to get me?" she asked, running her dry tongue nervously over her cracked lips.

"That depends."

"On what?" she asked.

"On you. Only you can make this choice. Do you want to stay and fight or..." He held out his hand for her to take.

~ ☾ ~

She could only stare at him. Death was really a choice? Somehow she doubted that.

She wanted him back so bad it hurt. But even as she reached out her hand to him, her fingers curled back. She couldn't leave. The girls needed saving more than she needed the sweet relief of death. And there was Jonah...

"Why have I been given a choice?" she asked.

"It's not your time. Not yet. These madmen don't deserve to change your fate. But I'm not saying either choice is an easy way out."

He paused, glancing up at the sound of one of those madmen shifting in a chair above them.

She took a deep breath, choking on tears she couldn't shed. "I'll stay."

"Good. I'm glad." His smile took her breath and broke her heart all over again. "These girls don't deserve to be trapped here. You can help them move on. You don't deserve to die."

"And you did?" The question escaped before she had a chance to think about it.

"Maybe I didn't deserve it, exactly, but it was my time. My work was done and I had to move on."

"What are you talking about?" she asked.

"Nothing. Don't worry about it. We need to focus on getting you out of this hole. That's what's important right now." He studied her prison walls.

"And a glass of water. I'd really like a glass of water."

"Alright," he laughed, helping her to stand. "We'll also focus on getting you a glass of water. You have to be strong though, Sloane. Find strength inside yourself. I can only help you so much. You're going to have to do the rest."

Head spinning, she wouldn't have stayed upright without him somehow holding her up. His words swam laps in her hazy mind. Tired and half dead, Sloane knew she had one trait that worked to her advantage right

~ ☽ ~

then. She was relentless. If given the chance, she would fight back and make her tormentors pay for what they'd done.

"Who are you talking to, bitch?" Glen craned his head over the edge of the hole. "I can hear you blabbing. You're always babbling even though no one is down there to listen to you. Still talking to those ghosts?"

There was a catch in his voice. Fear. He'd faced those ghosts. Hard to forget getting attacked by a gaggle of pissed off dead women. A growl rumbled in the air behind her as Ashley stepped through the wall into their mutual jail cell, still raging with revenge. Sloane couldn't wait to set her loose on Glen.

"He's not the brightest crayon in the box, is he?" Michael asked.

"Nope. And, much to his dismay, he's not even the most used."

"Hey." Glen tossed some peanut shells over the ledge. "I asked you a question." The shells scattered on the floor where they crunched.

"Get him down here," Michael snarled.

Sloane snorted. "Yeah, cause that went so well last time."

"Do it."

"How?"

"Make him mad."

Sloane sighed, steeling herself to follow his orders. But what would make him mad?

"Hey, Glen," she rasped into the intercom. "I'm ready for the incinerator."

"What?"

"Yeah, I'm tired of this game of cat and mouse and I'm sure you are too. You said yourself that I'm not very entertaining. Not like the other girls. Let's just get it over with."

"You want me to burn you?" Even she could hear the incredulity in his voice.

~ ☾ ~

"Yep."

"Don't listen to her, Glen." She heard Alvin's absurdly placating voice. She pictured him sitting in his chair, watching her slowly fade away on a video monitor with his smug, wrinkly smile.

Glen ignored him, his attention remaining riveted on Sloane.

"Don't tempt me," he called down.

"Why not? It worked once already. Or have you forgotten getting attacked by a flock of the girls you've tortured. You think their souls are singing on clouds or waiting patiently to destroy you? No, they want you now. Ashley says 'hi.' You wanted her, didn't you? She pissed you off so much that you didn't even wait till she was dead to dispose of her? Burned her alive. You totally trump Alvin on the sick and psycho chart. Your stupidity made her very powerful. How's that burn she gave you feeling?"

"You don't know what you're talking about," he said, rubbing at a burn on his arm.

"You wish I didn't know, but I do. I also met Lily. Your wife who 'ran away.'" Sloane made quotation marks with her fingers. "Does the whole town still believe that load of crap? You locked Alvin's little sister in the tunnel between the houses and starved her to death."

"He did what?" Alvin's face appeared over the side of the hole.

"No, I didn't," Glen insisted. "You know as well as I do your sister ran away with some other guy. She was a slut."

"I never should have believed you." Alvin put his head in his hands for a moment before rounding on Glen. "You killed Lily? You killed your wife, my beautiful sister? How could you?"

"Don't listen to her, Alvin," Glen pleaded. "You know the story. You know what happened."

~ ☾ ~

"I know what you told me," Alvin said. "You said you loved her and she left you."

"Ha," Sloane laughed. "You call that love? No wonder you didn't get anywhere with Karen. I saw her, old man. Beautiful, curly hair, a sad smile."

"She saw a picture," Glen insisted.

"She doesn't blame you Alvin," Sloane told him. "Even after all this time, she still wants to save you."

"You saw Lily? You really saw her? And she's dead?" Alvin's voice cracked. "All this time I thought she was out there somewhere, safe from us and what we've done. I was wrong."

"I told you not to listen to her," Glen yelled. "Now get back to your monitors. We have work to do."

"She thought you loved her, Glen." Sloane wouldn't let up. "And that love has turned to hate. She despises you. And hate is powerful. I wouldn't be surprised if she were the one to take you down in the end."

"Shut up, bitch. You don't want to make me angry."

"What are you going to do? Arrest me?" She laughed, a maniacal edge to her mirth. "Oh wait, you're the last one I should expect to follow the letter of the law. How did you get elected? Bribery? Blackmail? We sure as hell know you didn't sleep your way to the top."

"Shut up."

"Come down here and make me. I can't fight back. I can barely stand. Drag me up and put me in the damn fire already."

"I told you not to tempt me. I'll do it."

"Burn, baby, burn. Disco Inferno," she sang loudly and off key, leaning against the wall to keep her balance as she watched his face flame with rage. She was even slurring her words together like she was drunk. God, she wished she had a scotch and water. Hold the scotch. Heavy on the water.

Too much? Did it even matter if she got him down there? She spoke the truth. It's not like she could do

~ ☾ ~

anything about it when he did get the ladder down in the hole.

"Just be strong, Sloane," Michael whispered. "He is with you."

"Who is?"

"You know. You feel him. You've always felt him."

And she suddenly knew. It was Jonah.

It had always been Jonah!

Even when she been with Michael, she always had a sixth sense about Jonah. She always knew when he entered the room. Sometimes she even knew what emotion he was feeling. It wasn't something she could explain or even wanted to dwell on in her current state. Later. She just knew they had a connection and he would find her.

Jonah would find her. Was probably closer than she knew. He had to be. Because she could feel him. Feel him giving her strength. As much as she always wanted it to be Michael who would save her, Jonah was her knight in shining armor.

As if he heard her thoughts, she heard Jonah's voice. Muffled through the layers of insulation, but she could picture him there, prowling the tunnel, calling for her.

"Hell." Glen swore. "It's that damn FBI agent again. I thought you said calling that tip in would get rid of him."

"I thought it would, Glen. I swear." He coughed quietly.

A loud crack. Had Glen thumped Alvin in the back of the head?

"Obviously not, since he's here," Glen said. "You're worthless. You know that, right? Absolutely worthless. I can't wait until you kick the bucket. It's all I can do to keep from putting your sorry old, useless ass in the furnace now."

"S...s...sorry, Glen. I never expected someone to come

~ ☾ ~

looking for her." Alvin's voice was incredulous, like he couldn't believe someone would actually care enough to look for Sloane.

"Thanks a lot, Alvin!" she yelled up.

Even though Jonah was the only person who might mourn her, her ire rose. She wasn't that unremarkable, was she?

"What is he doing now?" Glen asked.

It was quiet for a moment, then Thump! Thump! Thump!

Not knocking like she was used to but the rhythmic boom of a sledgehammer hitting stone and wood. Jonah was trying to get in.

"You going to deal with the Fed?" Alvin asked.

"Yep," Glen answered. The rest of Glen's response faded beyond her hearing as he left the command center.

A heavy sigh pulled her attention back to where Michael lounged against the smooth concrete wall as though he usually spent his afterlife in sunken death pits.

"You were supposed to get him down in the hole."

"Excuse me," Sloane tried not to roll her eyes.

"I guess we're going to have to help you after all."

"And how are you going to do that?"

"We'll help you out of this hole."

She stared up at the fifteen foot lip. Even if she were hydrated and in shape, she could never reach that. Michael would have to work a miracle.

"Who is we?"

She should have known. The minute the words were out of her mouth, all of the women from Karen to Ashley stepped out of the walls, surrounding her.

"This ends with you," Karen said. "I thought you were lost, but you and your friend here convinced me I was wrong. That you are the one to break the cycle and end our torment."

~ ☾ ~

Michael concentrated on a point in the wall. He reached forward, his fingers sliding easily through the stone as he changed the makeup in the stone until there was a dip large enough to hold a hand or a foot. The light around him faded as he used his own spiritual strength to make a foothold.

The girls learned from his example. Each draining their power as they provided her with a means of escape.

"We can't do all the work," he told her. "But we can make it so it's possible to escape."

"Thank you," she breathed. Maybe, just maybe she could summon the strength to climb out. She was being given another chance to live.

"Don't thank us until you've made it to the top," Ashley breathed in her ear. "You still have a long way to go."

"Quick," Karen added. "While they're distracted."

Using the hand and foot holds they created for her, Sloane slowly made her way to the top, praying they were focused on Jonah and his attempt at rescuing her. Her ankle screamed with every step but she gritted her teeth to keep from crying out. Step by step she refused to relent. She prayed Alvin didn't see her and push her right back in. Or worse yet, have Glen deal with her after he killed Jonah.

Just before she reached the top, she paused, glancing back over her shoulder. Michael was still there, a sad smile on his face. He looked so lonely standing there. In his eyes she could see what might have been. The children they could have had, the laughter, the tears. All of it gone in the blink of an eye. And not just for her. He lost his hopes and dreams too.

"You were never supposed to be mine, you know."

"What?" she asked. "That's not true. I love you. You were the love of my life."

"No, Sloane. Not the love of your life, but a love. And that's enough for me."

~ ☾ ~

She stared at him, trying to deny what he said but knowing it was true.

"Thank you, Sloane. And tell Jonah thank you as well."

"For what?"

"For allowing me the chance to love you first."

She wanted to ask him what he meant, but at that moment, a shaft of light encompassed him and he disappeared, fading away to nothing, like sand caught in a summer wind and drifting off to sea.

Tears in her eyes, Sloane managed to pull herself over the lip of the pit and onto the flat ground beyond the hole.

Somehow she knew she'd never see Michael again. After all the waiting and the hoping she'd finally made contact with the other side. Now that she was a sensitive, many more battles were ahead but Michael wouldn't be a part of them.

His starring role was over and hers had just begun.

And the first of those battles involved a psychotic old man and his pathetic brother-in-law.

~ ☾ ~

CHAPTER 12

Alvin's wheelchair faced away from Sloane. Dumb luck. Quiet as a church mouse, she settled into a corner on the cool cement floor. Standing would take too much effort right now. She needed a minute to gather some strength. He hadn't noticed her...yet.

"Glen!" Alvin's voice crackled after him in a hoarse whisper. "Grab my pistol and kill that piece of shit FBI agent. He can rot in the hole with the girl. The gun's loaded and in the drawer next to my bed."

Glen muttered something about "a hole the size of Texas" in his skull from the tunnel before the door snapped shut behind him.

What time of night was it? What day was it? Sloane couldn't guess and didn't care. She had precious little time. Glen was on his way to kill an unsuspecting Jonah who pounded on a reinforced steel door that would only open if he found the trigger on the old recliner. She told him about the lever. Hadn't he found it yet? Here she was, all alone with psychopaths and her rescuer was stuck in the basement because he couldn't figure out how to use a recliner. Pain throbbed in Sloane's every cell and her biggest fight right now was staying conscious. Death was not just on her doorstep but had invited himself in and poured a cup of tea.

Heaving an internal sigh, she hauled herself to an upright position, propping herself against the wall. Glen's discarded glass of water sat within reach. The ice had melted and her eyes and mouth burned with greedy thirst. She snagged it.

~ ☾ ~

Giddy-up. It was just her and the old man.

"Don't you hate it when people don't pay attention," her voice was barely above a murmur and each spoken syllable burned her throat. Saliva was apparently a prerequisite for forming coherent words.

Alvin cranked the left rubber wheel back and right one forward until his wheelchair spun around to face her. His eyes widened in surprise for only a moment before returned to the bland indifference she so hated as he registered the fact she escaped.

Her hand shook violently as she brought the straw to her lips and sucked down the life-giving liquid. As soon as the cool liquid slid down her throat, her stomach promptly revolted and she threw it all back up into her lap. Repulsed by her own desires, she felt anger and pity for the ghosts once again. Her head propped against the wall behind her, she wiped the drool from her mouth and took deep breaths, meeting Alvin's dead eyes.

His face said it all. Burning hatred mingled with utter disregard for life. "Who helped you out?"

Reaching now for Glen's discarded soda can, she stuck her index finger under the tab and popped open the can. Carbonated fizzing sound filled the hidden room in between the sounds of Jonah's fast work with the sledgehammer. Sloane tried again, taking a deep swig of the warm beverage and wanting to scream in pain as the acidic contents burned every cell of her esophagus they encountered.

"I think you know the answer to that," she said.

Alvin straightened, his features made of stone. "No matter. Want to watch Jonah die?" He pointed his thumb to the wall with a video monitor of the hole and flicked a channel changer in his lap that he produced from under the red plaid flannel blanket that covered his legs.

It was Jonah all right; glistening with sweat attempting her rescue. It wouldn't take him long to get

~ ℂ ~

through the wall the way he was swinging that hammer. "My money is on Jonah 'cause your boss sucks ass."

Selfless Jonah. He'd sacrifice himself if it meant saving her and at that moment, she knew she would do the same.

"Are you sure about that?" Alvin asked, his bravado returned with Glen's absence. His eyes and head were sharp even if his body was not.

But the next frame on the monitor stopped her cold. Glen behind Jonah. Gun drawn.

"Behind you!" She intended to yell out the warning, but her weak voice was nothing more than a raspy whisper.

And then something in the video that shouldn't be there. A demon? A ghost! A version of Lily, her ghastly image flickering and nails out raced in a rage to attack Glen. She went right through him. Not enough energy for Glen to even feel her presence.

But it was enough to warn Jonah. In a split second, his expression changed and he redirected the sledgehammer that had hovered over his head. Instead of coming down on the wall, he spun around with such speed and force that it knocked Glen to the ground with one fell swoop.

"Told—" But before she could get out the word "you", Alvin had reached under his comfy blanket and produced a revolver of his own. He cocked it with his thumb and pointed it straight at her chest.

"No way I'm goin' to jail. I'm not going to die in some rat hole. I'm a free man."

Sloane put her hands up. "Hold up Alvin, no one said anything about jail. Glen was the perpetrator here. Not you."

"Pretty sure your FBI friend won't see it that way. So you'll both have to die and rot in that hole with Karen and the others."

Karen and the others. The image of Karen was strongest in Sloane's mind. She might have been a

~ ☾ ~

school teacher. Skirt properly ending below her knee, hair twisted into a subtle bun, hands reaching out to help Sloane. Her demeanor, even as a ghost was authoritative yet peaceful. She accepted this fate and helped the others pass into it as well. A tortured spirit leading others from a violent death into what might end up being—if Sloane didn't collect all her energy and find a way to fight—their perpetual anguish.

Sloane pictured Alvin trying in vain to woo Karen with flowers and candy. Had he knocked at her door politely at first? Or harassed her? Karen would have been nothing but kind to his advances. Maybe to her disadvantage. Her sweet sincerity the antithesis to the core of Alvin's being? Her courtesy the downfall for both? Had Alvin looked to Karen to save him from himself? And Karen couldn't find a hateful bone in her own body nor see the evil in others. Her innocence and purity being part of the reason she was mercilessly held hostage, tortured, and slain by monsters.

Did Alvin know about the ghosts all along?

Sloane had one card left to play. Rubbing her eyes with one hand, she stared at the empty wall behind Alvin feigning indignation. "No! No, he didn't say that Karen."

Eye wide as saucers, Alvin asked, "Is she here? Can you see her?" His head wheeled around and arms flailed into the air reaching for nothingness. Desperation seized him.

She continued. "Karen's been standing right behind you the whole time," she lied. Sloane edged a little toward the tunnel entrance Glen disappeared through. Alvin regained composure and never missed a beat. He retrained the gun in her direction. With this range, he'd hit something vital no matter what. "She wants me to talk for her."

"What's she saying?" Alvin's idea of love was twisted like a pretzel. "Tell me!" he demanded.

~ ☾ ~

"She wants you to die. She's pretty pissed Alvin."

And as fast as that, there were tears in Alvin's pathetic, wrinkled old eyes. "Tell her I loved her. I loved her so much that if I couldn't have her, then I needed to make sure no one else would have her either. See she *is* mine. I could always feel her here with me! Her anger kept me alive. Kept me listening to Glen, doing what he said...*killing those girls*," he whispered. "Each time I could feel Karen here with me. It was the only way to keep her close. Don't you see?" He threw his arms overhead waving the gun wildly. "Karen! I killed all the others for you! To keep you here with me!" Alvin again searched the room with wild eyes, gesticulating in every direction with a loaded weapon.

In a flash, Karen materialized. Right behind Alvin. All civility gone, she roared with anger. "So all this killing was my fault!" She lurched at him and moved his wheelchair a few millimeters.

Alvin sighed and threw his head back in smug laughter. "She is here! Tell her I felt that! I love her anger. It fuels me! Hatred is only a step away from love. She is close to loving me now that she understands what I've done for her. Doesn't she?"

Karen circled him like a shark spiraling around its prey looking for a weakness and opportunity to strike. Every time she lunged at him, he laughed harder, relishing her attentive rage he happily misconstrued as love. Karen was now the predator and Alvin the prey.

With Alvin occupied, Sloane moved another foot closer to the tunnel.

Karen's frustration mounted with her spirit's futile attempts to hurt him. Launching herself and anything else she could move fueled Alvin's bliss of otherworldly contact from his beloved.

Sloane was a stone's throw away from the door handle. She'd take her chances getting shot in the leg if Alvin even noticed she escaped.

~ ☾ ~

Alvin's eyes rolled back in his head. He turned the gun. At himself? Would he really take his own life to join Karen? Too bad he'd be in hell and she would finally rest in heaven. Sloane silently encouraged him. It would make her life easier.

Five feet from the tunnel door when Alvin snapped back to attention. "Tell me how she is moving. What she is saying! Is she asking me to join her? Finally?" The gun was pointed at Sloane once again. He didn't seem to notice her change of position.

"She is beautiful, Alvin. Just as you must remember her." At that exact moment, Karen's school teacher appearance that had so comforted Sloane morphed into something hideous. Her true form. Right before she died.

The Karen that Alvin created.

Sloane couldn't make eye contact with her. Rail thin and starved, blisters covered her mouth and oozed puss while her mouth foamed desperate for liquid. That which was once sweet, innocent Karen was rotting with dead eyes empty of hope and lustful with revenge.

"Girls. I need help. Now is the time. Girls!" Karen's screaming summoned the others who one by one clawed their way out of the pit. The entourage of rotting corpses arrived. Repulsed and trying to dry heave, Sloane prayed this clan could pool their powers and do some real damage.

Four feet from the tunnel.

Ashley pulled herself over the lip of the pit allowed herself to ignite in flames. She dove straight for Alvin, who relished the heat of her hate, welcoming his fiery tormentor with an embrace. Everywhere Ashley made contact, his skin blistered and charred.

"I feel the heat of your love my sweet Karen!" He clapped his hands with glee. "More! More!" He scratched at his blackened skin seemingly unfeeling of the pain from the body burns caused by Ashley. The

~ ☾ ~

girls crowded him, each clawing and scratching Alvin to try to exact revenge from their personal purgatories. "Beautiful. You think this is pain? Physical pain is nothing compared to what I've endured waiting for you my love!"

Three feet from the door. Alvin had gone mad.

The girls screamed and lunged from every angle causing far less damage in the physical world compared to the energy their spirits were using from their plane of existence. Alvin stretched out his arms, relishing every scratch. *Enjoying* it!

Two feet away. Time to make a break for it. She pulled down the handle and summoned all her remaining energy for the escape.

Three...two...

Whipping open the door, she slammed into Jonah—whose gun was pointed at Alvin.

"Put the gun down Alvin," he ordered. "You don't want to hurt anyone else now, do you?"

The ghosts retreated as Alvin once again snapped back to the reality of his current situation. Sloane held her breath. Although she was elated to see Jonah, she almost escaped and now Alvin's gun was pointed at Jonah and vice-versa. Shit. Double shit. A glance at the monitors showed something even worse. Glen's body was no longer lying on the floor of Alvin's basement.

Alvin wore a smile like a court jester; he was making a fool of them all. "As a matter of fact, I'm hoping to kill the both of you so I can feel Karen's wrath—love—whatever you want to call it, before I join her for all eternity."

"In her hell," Sloane said.

"And my heaven," countered Alvin.

"The only time you have left on this planet will be spent in a jail cell," Jonah said. "Or I could just send you to hell myself—without any of your victims I'm afraid. And either way jackass, I'm pretty sure you'll be

~ ☾ ~

completely alone." Jonah took one dangerous step closer while he flashed a glance behind Alvin directly at Karen's ghost. "I see we have company. She one of your victims?"

"Damn that both of you can see my beloved." Alvin turned his back to Jonah, set the gun in his lap and reached his arms out into the empty space.

Karen buried her face on her hands while backing away from him. "All this hatred. You let Glen use you all these years? Why not stand up for yourself? All to elicit a reaction from me? This is my fault! All the girl's murders were *my* fault. Their blood is on my hands!" She wept with dry eyes.

Jonah and Sloane stole a look. Sloane read his mind. His invisible hands squeezed her shoulders. She edged closer to him.

"You have one chance to make this right," Sloane offered.

"I know," Alvin and Karen answered in unison.

Jonah patted three fingers on his left thigh twice for Sloane to see. His signal meant move fast or be dead.

"Gig's up Alvin. Put the gun down," Jonah said.

Two fingers.

The girls surrounded Alvin fighting with each other for a chance to touch the wheelchair. Now it was Alvin who was five feet away from something... his own pit of torture.

One finger.

~ ☾ ~

CHAPTER 13

"Stop!"

Karen's scream broke through Alvin's maniacal laughter. Even he paused as if he could hear the dead woman's cry.

"No. I won't accept this." Her hands fisted at her sides gripping the fabric on her out-of-date gray pleated skirt. "I will not let him win. This is not my fault and he should pay for his sins."

As Sloane watched, the woman's eyes clouded with black until there were nothing left but eerie pits of darkness swirling inside her face. With a battle cry of rage, Karen threw her hands in the air, energy crackling around her.

One minute the sweet looking librarian type stood in the center of the room, the next she changed. Her rage focused until it caused her physical transformation. Her face contracted, a skeletal image pushing past her features, her nails elongating until the curved like claws. When she spoke there were multiple layers to her voice, as though more than one person spoke through her to deliver Alvin's sentence.

"You have sinned, Alvin Mitchell. You have shown wrath, greed, pride, lust, and envy and you have no remorse. You have been judged and deemed fit for purgatory and damnation. You will pay for these sins for all eternity."

With her gaze riveted on the ghostly woman, Sloane almost missed Alvin's reaction. As Karen spoke, her voice booming through the room, his eyes widened,

~ ☾ ~

body going rigid and nostrils were flaring with fear.

He'd been given the sight, she realized, and did not like what he saw. For the first time since he'd killed her, Alvin saw Karen. His wild eyes scanned the room. He saw all of them. All his victims. The lives he'd destroyed. Spirits who did not love him, but wanted him to pay.

They did not appear as they had to Sloane, where there was some semblance of the person they were before their death, but showed him exactly what he had helped to create. Dry cracked lips wept dark oozing blood in faces sunken as their eyes bulged, too big for their features. Skin sagged off bodies that were all bone, each and every piece of their skeleton visible.

They reached for him with boney hands, crying for his death as they closed ranks around him.

"No... no... no. This can't be happening." His voice cracked with fear as his gaze swiveled back to Karen. "You love me. I saved you from your sins. I haven't sinned myself. I know you love me. You have to."

"I never loved you. I could never love you." Karen's voice was firm, a knife cut to any man's soul. "How could anyone love a disgusting animal like you?"

"No, Karen, no." He fell from his chair, crawling toward the woman he'd fixated on his entire life until he was prostrate before her, begging for her love. "Don't you dare lie to me! Lying is a sin too. And you love me. I know you do."

He reached for her, but she stepped back, not allowing the contact.

"Death is too easy for you, old man," Karen said. "And my girls have so longed for their revenge."

As if her words were a cue, the ghostly victims reached for him. Wherever they touched, they drained the life from him, sucking it into themselves. They became more solid, their forms filling out, even as Alvin became even more drawn and emaciated than he'd been

~ ☾ ~

before. It didn't take long since he was already so close to death, before he looked as haggard and dehydrated as all of them.

He rolled onto his back, his breath coming in short, rasping gasps.

"Water," he whispered. "Please, water."

"There will be no water for you," Karen said. "You will suffer as we suffered. You are an abomination. A killer and a coward. You never deserved to be in this world with the rest of us. And now our torment ends…" An evil smile curved her blood red lips. "And yours begins."

She strode toward him, confident and determined as Sloane had never seen her.

Alvin raised his gun, pointing at her shadowy figure. Hand shaking, he squeezed the trigger.

Bang. Bang. Bang.

As the bullets fired, Jonah tackled Slone to the floor, shielding her body with his own. The bullets passed through Karen, embedding in the cold gray wall, until the gun was spent. Eyes wide with terror, Alvin inched backward, crawling away from his victims until he reached the edge of his pit. His muscles were weak so his movements were slow but the girls did not attack. They deliberately followed him, step for step, watching his fear grow.

"What are you doing?" Alvin used his wiry arms to shield his face as Karen loomed over him, the menacing skeleton still hiding her true features. Slowly the other girls surrounded him, hatred in their gazes as they condemned him as well.

"There's a dry hole in hell waiting for you," Karen told him softly, her voice and features slowly returning to her own. "And I hope you reap all you have sown."

Dark shadowy hands appeared, reaching from the pit, feeling their way along the cold cement sides until they found Alvin. Latching on, they pulled him backward, toppling him over the edge though he fought with all his

~ ☾ ~

might. His fingers caught the edge and he held on, trying to pull himself back out of the hole.

He searched the room, his eyes darting past Sloane fixing on something in the tunnel behind.

"Save me," Alvin begged.

"Why would I save you?" Glen sauntered into the room, his gun trained on Sloane. "You've done nothing but annoy me for years."

Even from his position, sprawled on the floor, Jonah trained his gun on the newcomer. Keeping their attention fixed on Glen and his gun, Jonah helped Sloane stand. He pushed her against the wall, backing away from Glen.

"But you're my partner," Alvin whined, his knuckles going white. "You're my friend."

"No." Glen switched his focus to the old man though his gun remained steady on Sloane. "You were the only one I'd ever met with a vendetta that would allow me to kill the way I wanted to. You gave me the opportunity, but you've served your purpose. I don't need you anymore."

Realization hit Alvin, his face crumbling, as he began to sob.

One of the shadowy hands reached over Alvin, grabbing the last of his thinning hair and pulled. His head jerked backward, the rest of his body following as he lost his grip on the ledge. He screamed as he fell, the blood curdling shrieks of someone who knew death awaited.

The cry continued after his body landed with a sickening splat, his screams going on and on as his soul was carried to the pits of purgatory.

"Well, that was unpleasant," Glen glanced around the room, his eyes resting on the army of ghosts. "You all look like hell, by the way. It's disgusting."

"You can see them?" Sloane asked.

"Your friend's hammer must have knocked a screw

~ ☾ ~

loose," Glen said. "So now I'll have to spend the rest of my life with them following me around, is that how this works?"

"If I had my way, that wouldn't be for very long," Sloane said.

"Ah, yes." His attention swiveled back to her. "The amazing Sloane Osborne. The only woman who's managed to escape the pit. I imagine they helped you, didn't they?"

She didn't feel the need to answer.

"I should shoot you now. And then your annoying boyfriend. Who knew an orphaned hermit like you would actually have someone care enough to come after you?" He moved the gun so it pointed at Jonah now. "Why couldn't you just leave it alone? If you had, none of this would have happened."

"I will always come for her," Jonah said. "If your research didn't tell you that, it was faulty."

"But you deserted her after Michael died. You should have been out of the picture."

"I did what she needed at the time," Jonah said.

"You ruined everything," Glen screamed. "Everything. Nothing will be the same again. I'll have to move. To rebuild. Start over and it's all your fault."

"No, you'll go to prison," Jonah's voice was calm. "You'll stay there until you die, then you'll join Alvin in hell."

"You first," Glen said, firing a shot without warning.

Sloane watched in horror, feeling as if the whole world was suddenly moving in slow motion. In the blink of an eye she saw her life without Jonah and it wasn't a life at all.

"No!" A woman screamed

Sloane dove in front of Jonah, feeling the bullet tear through the skin in her shoulder, before she fell to the ground at his feet. Jonah knelt beside her, pulling at the collar of her shirt to expose the wound.

~ ☾ ~

"You're ok." He laid a hand on her cheek. "It just grazed you. Stay down." He used his body to shield her from the rest of the room.

The woman's voice echoed from the depths of the tunnel.

"You will not kill again!"

Lily stepped into the room.

She was no longer the sad, distracted woman Sloane had met in the corridor, but looked more like a demon-possessed warrior. Her skin was glowing with a reddish tinge, her face a skeleton mask of hate. Black soulless eyes fixed on Glen and she smiled showing sharp, pointed teeth.

"Lily," Glen gasped, his eyes widening in shock.

"I've had a lot of time to think while I was in the tunnel," Lily said. "And I realized something."

Glen sputtered incoherently but the ghost didn't notice. She didn't even notice when he trained his gun on her either.

"I realized that more than being finally allowed to enter the gates of heaven, more than seeing you in hell, I wanted you to suffer as I suffered."

"You want him to starve in the tunnel?" Jonah asked.

"I want him to know the pain of a husband who hates you, who beats you, and makes you have sex with him, even when you want to vomit at the thought. I want him to feel the shame of regret. I want him to die in the most painful way possible and relive it again and again."

"To do this, you would give up your own chance of salvation." Karen made her way past the watching army to rest a hand on the possessed woman's shoulder. "If you give into your evil, you will suffer the same fate as him."

Lily's eyes fixed on Karen and for a moment Sloane was sure she saw regret in her eyes.

"I've come to terms with that," she said. "I deserve this fate. I suspected and I did nothing because I was afraid."

~ ☾ ~

"This was no more your fault than mine, dear," Karen said.

"I made my deal long ago," Lily said. "I didn't have the same support group as you. Maybe if I had, I would choose differently, but I've spent too long alone and all I want is *him*."

Reaching out, her nails elongated until they were sharp, cruel claws. She moved quicker than the eye could see and in only a moment, she batted the gun out of Glen's hands, and digging her claws into his chest, raised him into the air. Blood dripped from the puncture wounds, draining down onto her face and she licked at the drops with her tongue.

"You taste of fear," she growled.

"Lily, sweetie, you don't want to do this," Glen screamed. "Just let me go. I'll do whatever you want."

"You'll do whatever I want now."

Quick as lightning she dragged his squirming form into the tunnel. When his scream finally faded into the distance, shafts of light began to appear around each of the girls. Gorgeous beams of sunlight glimmering through the cement walls into the hidden basement room. One by one each of the ghosts stepped into the light, disappearing into the shimmering rays.

The last to go was Karen, now back to her schoolmarm image, who turned to Sloane, blowing one last kiss before the light enveloped her in its loving embrace.

Jonah lifted Sloane into his arms as their gaze met, his brown eyes wide. The pain her adrenaline had conquered pushed itself back to the forefront as her entire body throbbed in pain.

"Did that really just happen?" he asked.

She nodded.

"I can't believe you took a bullet for me."

"You're worth it," she managed as the heavenly darkness descended and Sloane welcomed the numbness it provided.

~ ☾ ~

Wind whistled past her face, chilling her cheeks and making her dark hair dance around her too pale face. Sloane knew she should still be inside, recovering, but she had to come here. Had to feel the cold, hard ground seeping into her shoes as she stood on the still green grass and said good-bye.

There was nothing of Karen in the grave. She knew that, but it was the only place she could think to go. She didn't want to go to the house. She never wanted to go there again. So instead she was in a graveyard, trying to sort her thoughts.

She could still hear the machines, beeping around her though she been release from the hospital over an hour ago. It had been a long two weeks, harder on Jonah than her. She just had to rest, recover, and drink. Oh, glorious water. Sloane knew she would never take it for granted again. She was planning on drinking gallons a day for the rest of her life.

The first few days in the hospital had been a bit of a blur as she drifted in and out of consciousness but one thing she knew for certain; Jonah never left her side. He'd held her hand, read to her, and even kissed her forehead as he brushed hair off her face.

He'd also talked. A lot. About things she wasn't sure she was meant to remember. But she did. She'd never forget. How could she?

It had always been a joke between the three of them: Michael, Jonah and her, about how Michael had won her in a coin toss when he and Jonah had first seen her in that bar. It was true. They'd flipped a coin to see who could make the first move and Michael had won.

She always been so grateful he'd won because she loved Michael with all her heart and soul. A piece of her always would though, somehow, she knew he was gone. He'd made contact here and helped her, but he

~ ☾ ~

wouldn't do it again. Like the girls, he'd moved on. She had to accept it.

But what had sent her into the graveyard this morning wasn't Michael's spirit, but her own. She needed a friend to talk to and, sadly, the worn gray stone reading Karen Hartwell, beautiful daughter, was as close as she'd come.

"It was a lie. All of it," she whispered. "Jonah won the coin flip but had known, somehow had just known, Michael needed his chance first. How could he have known?"

She could still feel Jonah's warm hands enveloping hers as he'd broken the news. He'd thought he was safe, that she was unconscious, but she been drifting somewhere between sleep and awake and had heard. Had understood.

He'd seen the possessive gleam in Michael's eyes the moment she walked in the room and had known no matter how he felt, he didn't stand a chance. And there'd never been anything he'd regretted more.

"How's someone supposed to react to that?" she asked. Only the wind answered.

But deep down she knew. All she had to do was let go of Michael. Keep his memory, of course, but let go and once she did her heart would bloom like a summer rose.

And she also knew what she'd find there. Love. Blossoming and growing.

"I needed to love Michael first," she told the gray stone. "To prepare me for Jonah's love. And he does love me. I know it, even if we both aren't ready for that love yet."

Soon, she knew, but she needed more time before they could be together.

Soft footsteps flattened the grass behind her. She didn't need to turn to know he stood there, close enough to almost touch. The connection between

~ ☾ ~

them had grown stronger. She could sense him. Knew him as well as she knew herself.

Without turning, she reached back for his hand, threading his warm fingers through her own.

"Have you said what you needed to?"

She shrugged. "I guess I have. I really just came to talk things out and I've done that."

"Found your answers then?" He stepped forward, his heat seeping through her light jacket and into her skin.

Turning, she looked into his eyes. He really was handsome and charming in a white knight sort of way.

On an impulse she reached up onto her tiptoes and pressed her lips to his. For a moment, he hesitated, stiffening before he relaxed into her, wrapping an arm around her waist and pulling her close. She opened to him and his tongue plundered inside, dueling with hers.

She meant this kiss as a gesture, maybe a test, to see what it would be like to kiss her best friend. She expected it to be nice, maybe even arousing, but suddenly, she was on fire.

She melted into him, her hands tunneling into the softness of his hair as she pulled him closer, wrapping herself in his essence until she didn't want to let go.

It was Jonah who broke the kiss first, but he kept the contact, keeping her wrapped in his arms.

"Thanks for saving me," she whispered against his chest.

"I'll always save you." His voice was gruff. "Though I'd appreciate it if I didn't have to do it again anytime soon."

She laughed, pulling away to take in the laugh lines around his eyes and the slight dimple in his right cheek.

"So what now?" He turned her towards his car, fitting her under his arm as they walked together.

"Now? I guess I've kind of been working on a day to

~ ☾ ~

day. I haven't thought about what to do next. I suppose I need to get back to work though. Selling haunted houses."

"Any leads?" There was a gleam in his eyes that should have worried her but instead she felt a smile spread across her face.

"What do you know?" she asked.

"Well, there's this house in Maine. My friend is calling in a debt but I think it's right up your alley. It's an old place, of course, with lots of history. Including a disaster of some sort."

"I do love a good disaster. Are there interested buyers?"

"No, this house isn't for sale."

Sloane frowned, glaring at him. Why would she want to go somewhere else she wouldn't get paid?

"My friend and his new wife found they're dream house but are having some trouble. They're willing to pay top dollar to find out what's going on in this house."

"Then I guess I'm headed to Maine."

~ ☾ ~

ACKNOWLEDGEMENTS

We'd like to thank Stephanie Murray and Marlene Castricato at Crescent Moon Press for believing in our book, as well as the superb editing skills of Kerry Genova, who has made it shine.

Thanks a million to Jody Nordby, our beta reader extraordinaire. We appreciate everything you do for us! And a big thank you to our paranormal experts: Jim and Stephanie.

R. A. Green would like to thank Kat de Falla for being an inspiration and guiding light. For pushing me to go beyond what I knew I could do and being a great friend. Also, thanks to my husband for loving and believing in me, even when I disappear to write all day with Kat. Thanks to my two amazing children for allowing mommy to have a time out with the computer. And to my parents and in-laws for all their support.

Kat de Falla would like to thank Rachel for being more than a writing partner and friend, but someone who's pushed me to become a better person. Also, thanks to my four beautiful children, parents and sister for always supporting my writing. And above all, I thank my muse, soul mate, and husband. A man made of stardust and dreams that turned out to be flesh and blood and not a mere figment of my imagination: Lee is the summit of my life's hopes and dreams. Without him, there is no success as only when he is by my side, is my life complete. I love you Lee! My love, loyalty, and friendship is yours alone.

ABOUT THE AUTHOR

Kat Green is the dynamic writing duo of R. A. Green and Kat de Falla.

Author R. A. Green's upcoming debut novel is First Contact, Book One of the Sloane Osborne Haunts for Sale Series that she co-wrote with Kat de Falla as Kat Green. It will be released in 2014 by Crescent Moon Press. She is also an editor of Romance Flash. She is an avid Disney fan who lives with her husband and two young children in Wisconsin. She owns an in-home daycare so all of her writing gets done in short spurts during nap time.

Author Kat de Falla was born and raised in Milwaukee, Wisconsin where she learned to roller skate, ride a banana seat bike, and love Shakespeare thanks to her high school English teacher. Four years at the UW-Madison wasn't enough, so she returned to her beloved college town for her Doctor of Pharmacy degree and is happily employed as a retail pharmacist where she fills prescriptions and chats with her patients. She is married to her soul mate, classical guitarist, Lee de Falla, and raising four kids together ala the Brady Bunch.

Kat Green's Website: www.hauntsforsale.com
Kat de Falla's Website: www.katdefalla.com
R. A. Green's Website: http://rgreen1017.wix.com/ragreen
Kat's Blog: www.quillorpill.blogspot.com
R. A. Green's Blog: http://authorragreen.blogspot.com/
Follow us on Facebook
at: www.facebook.com/authorkatgreen
Follow us on Twitter at; www.twitter.com/@hauntsforsale

ADDITIONAL INFORMATION

Please visit www.bayafaya.com for FREE music downloads
that accompany this book.

CPSIA information can be obtained at www.ICGtesting.com
Printed in the USA
BVOW04s0756191214

379976BV00001B/59/P